GW00750520

Love is
a time of enchantment:
in it all days are fair and all fields
green. Youth is blest by it,
old age made benign: the eyes of love see
roses blooming in December,
and sunshine through rain. Verily
is the time of true-love
a time of enchantment—and
Oh! how eager is woman
to be bewitched!

ONE WHO REMEMBERS

Why should Constant Smith remember the Decointres so vividly when they had deliberately lost touch with her? Since her mother's death, Constant had been doing private nursing. Now she had a chance to break back into the Decointres' lives as nurse to the young heiress, Katy, who was to be Aylward's bride. Aylward, who was her childhood's hero and champion. Could she school herself to meet them again and yet, how could she resist the temptation?

Books by Theresa Charles
in the Ulverscroft Large Print Series:

THERESA CHARLES

ONE WHO REMEMBERS

Complete and Unabridged

ULVERSCROFT
Leicester

First published in Great Britain in 1976

First Large Print Edition
published September 1988

British Library CIP Data

Charles, Theresa
    One who remembers.—Large print ed.—
    Ulverscroft large print series: romance
    Rn: Irene Maude Swatridge and Charles
    John Swatridge   I. Title
    823'.914[F]

    ISBN 0-7089-1862-X

Published by
F. A. Thorpe (Publishing) Ltd.
Anstey, Leicestershire
Set by Rowland Phototypesetting Ltd.
Bury St. Edmunds, Suffolk
Printed and bound in Great Britain by
T. J. Press (Padstow) Ltd., Padstow, Cornwall

1

"Under a spreading chestnut tree,
The village smithy stands."

H. W. LONGFELLOW

"WHAT do you intend to do now? Find another dead-end job, looking after another elderly, eccentric invalid?" Belle demanded, not challengingly but resignedly, as if she were already aware of the answer.

Her chilly, half patronising, half scornful gaze flickered over me, withering my impulse to confide in her. I hadn't seen her for over a year, but she hadn't changed. She would never change in her attitude towards me.

I couldn't remember that she had ever been actively unkind. If she hadn't attempted to conceal the resentment she had felt when her widowed mother had married my father, she had, even as a child, been too logical to extend that resentment to the helpless baby who had arrived a year later. Some little girls of five would have welcomed and mothered a baby sister, but Belle wasn't maternally minded. Perhaps, after she had been the sole object of Mother's attention, she couldn't have been expected to share Mother willingly with Father and me.

She hadn't, I thought, resented Father himself. Who could have cherished any bitter feelings against that big, genial, easy-going, essentially lovable man, Dallas Smith? He had been "hail-fellow-well-met" with the whole village. It hadn't been the man but his calling which had stuck in my half-sister's throat. In our schooldays, she had been absurdly sensitive to any teasing references to "the village blacksmith". She had insisted that she was Belinda Benson and not "the village blacksmith's daughter".

I had been puzzled and hurt by her reaction. I hadn't understood why she couldn't share my warm pride in my father and his craft. The Forge had been his father's and grandfather's and great-grandfather's. He was dedicated to his calling, and to the family tradition. He shod ponies and horses, as his ancestors had done, but Father had been an artist as well as a farrier. His wrought-iron work had been in great demand.

Mother's family traditions, bragged of by Belle, had seemed to me dull and ordinary. Mother's father and grandfather had been doctors. Mother had been a nurse in a City hospital when she had met and married the young doctor who had been Belle's father. It had been as a District Nurse that Mother had come to Netherfield Green—and captivated "the village blacksmith", during the professional visits she had paid to the Forge to dress a burned leg.

Mother had taken it for granted that her daughters would train as nurses in due course. Belle had passed her exams with consummate ease and was now a highly respected Sister at a big Plymouth hospital. I had barely completed two years' training when Father's sudden, tragic death—from a kick on the temple from a mettlesome horse he had been shoeing—and Mother's subsequent collapse, from hitherto unsuspected heart trouble, had made it imperative that either Belle or I

3

must stay at home to look after her. Belle was at that time a Staff Nurse at St. Cyriac's, our training hospital on the Surrey–Sussex borders—and had just applied for and obtained a better-paid job in Plymouth. It had been unthinkable that she should abandon her promising career. It hadn't been much of a wrench to abandon mine, since my dreams were all of Cecil and of the future we would share . . .

"You ought to go back to St. Cyriac's and take your finals," Belle said, in a tone as crisp as the salad to which I was helping myself. "Why on earth don't you?"

"I'm twenty-five. Nearly twenty-six," I reminded her. "I should feel a fool, having to start all over again. I don't think I'd ever get used to hospital life now, either. Besides, it isn't as if there weren't plenty of jobs available."

"Wretchedly unrewarding, dreary jobs," Belle said critically. "To bury yourself in the depths of the country, with some old lady who can barely make ends meet, is the height of futility. All wrong at your age."

"I like the country and I like looking

4

after old ladies," I said defensively. "At least, I liked living with Henrietta Pearson. She was a darling; cheerful and indomitable to the last. I found acting as her secretary quite absorbing. We used to discuss her characters and plots."

"Enthralling! I can imagine . . ."

I felt myself flushing. It was no use. I couldn't hope to make Belle understand why I had been happy, in that lonely cottage on the Cornish cliffs, with Henrietta Pearson and her old cook-housekeeper, three plump cats, and a lively dachshund.

"Three years' drudgery—and what have you to show for it?" Belle asked, after a pause. "Miss Pearson didn't even leave you the cottage, did she?"

"I didn't expect anything from her," I said hurriedly. "It was only fair that she should have left the cottage and an annuity to old Martha, who'd been her cook-housekeeper for thirty years. Miss Pearson did leave me her car and some personal possessions. That's why her solicitors want to see me, and I'm on my way to London."

"A few old-fashioned trinkets, I

suppose? And a car which you can't afford to run," Belle said disparagingly. "Why can't you make something of your life before it's too late?"

Make what? I wondered rebelliously, regretting my impulse to stop off in Plymouth to lunch with Belle.

I glanced round the sitting-room. Belle's flat was a reflection of herself; lovely but austere. The white walls, the deep grey carpeting, the ice blue curtains and chair covers, the good but sparse furniture and the absence of any feminine "clutter", formed an appropriate background for Belle's tall, supple figure, sleek, shining fair hair and delicately chiselled features.

Years ago, the Decanters had nick-named her "La Belle Blonde", after one of their mother's favourite roses, but to me Belle resembled a tulip rather than a rose; "fresh without fragrance", and "half metal", in Humbert Wolfe's telling lines.

Had it been the Decanters who had first made her conscious of a need for armour? If they had never come to Netherfield Green, never cantered up to the Forge, gay, lively, and demanding, to cast a spell over me and to antagonise my sister, would she have blossomed without that hint of frost about her? Should I have become more of a doer and less of a dreamer?

With the age gap between us, I had been virtually an only child. I had been seven years old when the Squire had died. To the local children, he had been a legendary figure, rarely glimpsed, even on our daring forays into the grounds of De Cointreaux Hall, in search of fallen apples or chestnuts. On these forays, we had stalked and dodged him as if he had been a ferocious ogre. In actual fact, he probably wouldn't have noticed us, had he caught us with bulging pockets. From my parents' conversation, I had gathered that ever since his only son had been killed in the War, the Squire had withdrawn behind his high stone walls and into the existence of an elderly recluse. My mother, still the responsible District Nurse at heart, had thought it "terrible for the poor old man to cut himself off from his remaining kith and kin, just because of a stupid family quarrel when he was a boy. There ought to be a reconciliation before it's too late. Can't the Vicar reason with him?"

7

"My love, nobody can reason with a Decointre. D'you suppose the Vicar hasn't tried? And Dr. Coburn-Macdonald's tried, too. It's not a bit of use," Father had told her. "The family motto means 'Never Forget'. If the estate wasn't entailed, the Squire would have disinherited his cousin's son, years ago."

I could barely remember that lean, wiry, white-haired old man, and yet his death had changed my whole life pattern. I was only mildly interested by the rapidly circulating village gossip about the new Squire, who had, it was rumoured, been living on and running a ranch in Canada. It was reported that he was selling the ranch, and bringing his wife and family to De Cointreaux Hall. At school, one of the more imaginative children hinted that the new Squire was black—which was why he had been kept as a dark secret all these years. Others insisted that he had married a Red Indian squaw, and that their offspring would ride around with feathers in their hair, brandishing tomahawks.

"What nonsense!" Belle said scornfully, when I repeated the rumours to her. "They'll be able to ride, no doubt, if

the deferential way in which he leaned towards me, waiting for my answer.

"Yes," I said breathlessly. "Yes. I do like it better."

"Conker's short for Conqueror, so it's not appropriate. A girl can't be a conqueror . . ."

The protest came from his brother, whom, until then, I had barely noticed. He had stayed in the background, while Angela had been introducing herself and her twin. He was smaller and thinner, his hair a mousy brown, and his tan several shades lighter. His features were less boldly defined, and he was wearing rounded glasses which gave him the look of a young owl.

"She can—so there! What about 'She Stoops to Conquer', Mr. Clever?" Angela flashed. Then, jerking her head towards her younger brother, she announced: "He's Cecil. He's only eight, but he thinks he's the brains of the family and knows all the answers."

"I'm nearly nine—and I've won more prizes than Aylward has," Cecil reminded her.

"Oh, granted! You're the Brain. I'm merely the Brawn," Aylward grinned.

His eyes were fringed with exaggeratedly long black lashes, like a young calf's, and there was a charm I had never before encountered in his smile. When he smiled, lights danced in his eyes, and crinkles appeared at the corners of them, and his lips quirked upwards, revealing strong, sparkling white teeth. He gave me the feeling that all was well with the world, and always would be, while he was in the picture.

Did I gather those vivid impressions in that first encounter, or afterwards, more gradually? Difficult to remember now, nearly twenty years later, though the scene itself was engraved indelibly on my memory; with its scents and sounds. The scents—hawthorn and horse-chestnut, fire, and warm clean horse, made an unforgettable combination; a familiar combination but one which had never registered on me so deeply before. The sounds—the jingle of harness and restless movements of the ponies' feet—had been dominated by Angela's voice, high-pitched and imperious, as she had fired questions at me. She was, it seemed, puzzled and aggrieved because the local farmers were so "kind of unfriendly", ordering the three newcomers off their land. Where in this "one horse town" could one ride?

In graphic language, she described recent encounters with irate farmers. I gaped at her, shocked by the ignorance of so dazzling a being. Didn't she know that in May certain fields were shut up for hay, and that it was a cardinal offence to ride over them before the hay was cut? It was even more of a crime to ride over the young, growing corn.

"What did I tell you?" Cecil demanded triumphantly, when I had tried to explain.

"Mr. Clever!" Angela grimaced at him and appealed to me again. "Then, where can the ponies let off steam?"

There was the common and there were old, established bridle-paths, I told her. In her gay, imperious fashion, she insisted that I must ride with them and show them. By the time her pony's missing shoe had been replaced and the three of them rode away, heading back to the Hall, I had lost my heart, finally and irrevocably, to the Decanters.

They were always "the Decanters" to me and to the other village children. The family name had originally been De Cointreaux. At some time in the distant past, probably during one of England's periodical wars with France, the family had anglicised De Cointreaux into Decointre. I suppose "Decanter" was easier for childish tongues and certainly more appropriate to such skilled horsemen. Angela and Aylward rode as if born to the saddle. Cecil was more cautious and less of what Belle called a "show-off". I could admire Angela's verve and élan, but my father's training made me secretly wince from her recklessness and occasional lack of consideration for her pony. I never ventured to criticise her openly. I learned early that Angela wouldn't tolerate criticism or rebellion. Having welcomed me into the family circle, she expected the same unquestioning allegiance from me as from her brothers. In return, she treated me as she treated Cecil. We had to be kept in our places, but she was swift to protect us from outsiders . . .

It was May again now. I had glimpsed horse-chestnuts in flower as I had driven

16

through St. Austell, and in the country hedgerows hawthorn had been bursting into blossom. Gorse was still ablaze, and primroses still starred the banks, with wild violets and stitchwort. In Netherfield Green, the woods around the Hall would be carpeted by bluebells.

May to me was the queen of the year; an enchanted month, with all the delights of spring, and also the rich promise of summer. May was a month of long—ever lengthening—light evenings, and a crystal clear air, peculiarly her own, of hot sunshine, variable, but rarely tempestuous winds, and a delicious sense of antici-pation, of "the best is yet to be". Perhaps, that far-off May when I was seven years old, and the golden vistas it had opened before me, had made me love the month for ever.

To be one of a family, if only the youngest and least important, had been like a cherished dream come true. No more long, lonely hours during school holidays. From that evening when they had first come to The Forge, my whole life had centred round the Decanters. I was included in all their plans as a matter of course. Instead of catching a bus into the market town to school, I was driven there, with my new friends, by the Squire or his wife.

Belle was the one cloud on my shining horizon. Almost from the first, she and Angela clashed. That Belle was two years older didn't help her to maintain her position at school in the face of Angela's determined challenges. Angela was instantly popular and obviously a born leader. I was content to follow her lead. I was bewildered when Belle inveighed against "that girl's insufferable conceit and bossiness".

I was small, red-haired and freckled, with no great opinion of my own looks or brains. Belle, at twelve, was already a beauty in her cool, pastel, lily-like fashion. For the past two summers, she had been chosen as the town's "Fair Week Queen". In the summer of the Decanters' arrival, that title was bestowed upon Angela. It was Angela, not Belle, who was given the star part in the school's end of term play . . .

Belle had always been reserved, "stuck up" some of the village children called her.

Angela was a naturally good mixer, and a natural eye-catcher, with her warm vitality, striking good looks, and irrepressibly high spirits. Years later, I could understand how Belle must have suffered, and why she resented Angela as a usurper. At the time, I was merely sorry for her disappointments, and sorrier that she persistently held aloof from the Decanters.

Mother and Mary Decointre were soon firm friends, and so Belle couldn't count on much sympathy from Mother, who was wont to chide her briskly: "You can't always expect to come first, darling. Angela is the Squire's daughter. It's natural that she should take a leading part in local activities. You needn't be hurt about it. Do I mind because Mary Decointre has been elected the new Chairman of our WI? Does Father feel aggrieved because the Squire has been chosen as the new Chairman of the Parish Council? Of course not. We're lucky to have an active Squire and his wife here."

Belle couldn't see it that way. She wasn't old enough or worldly wise enough to make allowances for the proverbial fickleness of any public, large or small.

Belle went on cherishing grievances against the Decanters, deriding their easy popularity, and affecting to scoff at their ambitions. They were all three resolved to make their mark, and they saw no reason to be reticent about their objectives.

Aylward, as adventurous in his own way as his twin, was going to be a famous explorer and naturalist. He was going to track down rare birds and animals and plants. Not to shoot or even to capture them, he would explain earnestly; just to prove how and where they survived. Angela, who was keen on photography, planned to accompany him on his expeditions and to film the results . . . which would make them both world famous. Cecil and I could tag along with them, as doctor and nurse, Angela would add kindly.

Cecil, inevitably overshadowed by his more spectacular brother and sister, had no apparent yearning for the limelight. He was going to be a doctor, like his mother's father, who had his own highly successful and celebrated clinic in Montreal. He was going to discover cures for diseases which had hitherto baffled the medical profession. Cecil, though I hadn't realised it for years, had as much self-confidence as the twins, and was equally determined to make a name for himself.

I must have been nine years old when it dawned on me that our quartette wasn't permanent and indissoluble. It was on a cold, crisp December evening. The four of us were gathered around the vast hearth of the dining-room at the Hall, roasting chestnuts gathered in the woods. There was some fortune telling rite attached to the roasting, and Angela was protesting that, by allowing Aylward to place my chestnuts in position for me, I wasn't playing fair.

"Don't tease the child! She has singed her paws already," Aylward intervened, with one of those flashes of protective chivalry which kindled the fires of hero worship in me. "Besides, she doesn't need to have her fortune foretold. Girls with her chestnut coloured hair and cat green eyes are born witches. She'll get whatever she wants out of life."

"And what's that?" the Squire asked idly, from his armchair at the edge of our semi-circle. "What do you want from life, my dear? A title, a handsome husband, and £10,000 a year?"

"Oh, no! I just want to marry Aylward, and go on his expeditions with him," I answered unhesitatingly.

Aylward bowed and said lightly: "Thank you, sweetheart!" but Cecil looked at me reproachfully, and Mary Decointre, swift to sense his hurt, protested: "Aylward? What about Cecil? I thought you were Cecil's special pal."

"Oh, yes!" I said, in flurried remorse. "I love Cecil just as much. I'll marry him, too."

That evoked general laughter, until Angela said purposefully: "You can't marry Aylward. He'll have to marry an heiress who'll finance our expeditions. You'll have to settle for C."

"You will, too," Cecil told me with grave determination. "You and I belong together."

From the first, I had been fascinated by Aylward, but Cecil, nearer my own age, was my faithful ally and companion.

When he said seriously: "I love you and he doesn't. Promise that you'll marry me some day—" I said resignedly: "All right. I will."

"That's a promise," he insisted.

Ten years later, when we were both students at St. Cyriac's, he held me to it, and we became unofficially engaged. We knew it would be a long engagement, but we were prepared to wait. Life had been full of promise for all of us in those days.

The others had forged ahead—were still forging ahead—in pursuit of their dreams. It had been I alone who had seen my castle in the air collapse like a child's house of cards. Or, no. Nothing as dramatic as a sudden collapse. My dreams had subsided gradually, like a sand castle that was being encroached upon and washed away by the incoming tide. There was no point at which I could have cried out in anguish: "It's all over. Cecil doesn't love me any longer."

He had never said that he had ceased to love me; never admitted that he had grown weary of waiting. He had just, almost imperceptibly at first, begun to drift away from me. His visits, always brief, had become briefer, with longer intervals between them. He was working hard, and the two hundred miles drive down to Plymouth was exhausting, particularly in the tourist season. It would be selfish of me to expect him to struggle through the inevitable hold-ups in the holiday traffic simply in order to spend a few hours with me. He would do better in the autumn. Then, when the autumn had come, a wild and stormy autumn, there had been the weather to contend with and consider. Any forecast of snow, icy roads, or thick fog, and Cecil hadn't dared to risk being stranded.

He would spend Christmas with me and Mother in the small bungalow Belle had found for us . . . unless I could induce Belle to look after Mother and join the family at the Hall? His parents hoped that might be possible. The Squire hadn't been too fit, and his mother wanted him at home to keep an eye on his father. Would Belle have stepped into the breach and let me escape for a few days? I was never to know, because both Belle and Mother went down with 'flu, and I had to spend that Christmas nursing them . . .

Letters were some consolation, but not much. I wrote frequently and from my heart, but Cecil couldn't apparently express himself freely on paper. In all those long drawn out months of our engagement, I never once received a really impassioned love letter from him; the kind of letter to be locked away from prying eyes and cherished for years ahead.

Yet I had never doubted his love for me; never doubted that, if he had been in a position to assume the responsibility of a wife and a semi-invalid mother-in-law, he would unhesitatingly have named the day. That he might resent what he called my "devotion" to my mother, didn't occur to me. I had never felt especially close to my mother. I had from an early age been "Daddy's girl".

I couldn't pretend that any deep, devoted love made me willing to sacrifice my future for my mother. I had been thrust into the job of looking after her by Belle. I hadn't expected it to last indefinitely. After all, Mother was only in her fifties. I supposed that, with rest and care, her heart condition would improve. Perhaps most of us are inclined to take our parents for granted. Certainly, I had never consciously studied my mother as an individual. I hadn't guessed that she was essentially a "man's woman". She had had two happy marriages and two devoted husbands. Now, widowed for the second time, and in failing health, with only a young daughter, deep in her own dreams, for company, Mother lost all interest in life. Why make an effort, when there was no man around to appreciate and encourage her?

To my dismay, she became increasingly dependent on me. Belle, to be fair to her, did her best to persuade Mother to "stop pitying yourself and snap out of it". Unluckily, she merely convinced Mother that her elder daughter was hard and unsympathetic. Consequently, Mother clung even more tightly and demandingly to me. Could I have foreseen the result, would I have had the courage—or the callousness—to have broken away from her?

As it was, the crisis arrived suddenly and without warning. Cecil, having completed his stint as a junior houseman at St. Cyriac's, had been invited to spend the next two years at his grandfather's celebrated Clinic in Montreal. It was an opportunity he couldn't afford to turn down, especially in view of the fact that his father's death, two months previously, had revealed a grave financial morass. Aylward, who had been down from Cambridge for six months and had been struggling to get the estate out of the red, was planning to let the Hall. Angela had already left home and had been working in a studio in London for the past two years.

"The Hall's a complete white elephant. We can't sell it, worse luck, but we may be able to let it. Mother will be quite comfortable at the Lodge, and Aylward will be living with her. There's nothing to keep me here," Cecil told me frankly. "Grandfather's getting on now, and I'd like to work with him before he retires."

"Of course," I said wretchedly. "But . . . what about me?"

"That's up to you! We could be married quietly and you could come with me. That's what I would like," he assured me. "But . . . my wishes don't seem to count for much with you, in comparison with your mother's."

That was the first time I had realised

that Cecil was secretly and bitterly jealous of my mother's claims on me. I had been startled and shocked by the revelation.

"It isn't true that she comes first with me," I protested. "It's simply that she isn't fit to be on her own. Someone has to look after her."

"Then, let your sister do it."

"Belle won't give up her job . . . and Mother wouldn't be happy with her, anyway. How can I leave her?"

I was confused and distracted, torn between my love for Cecil and Mother's dependence on me. That Cecil failed to grasp my predicament came as a slap in the face. I had adored him and his whole family for so long; had indeed felt that I was one of them, ever since I was seven. It didn't seem possible that Cecil could suddenly dissociate himself from me, and banish me from that charmed circle.

He didn't present me with an ultimatum, or I might have silenced my conscience and thrown the onus for Mother's welfare on my sister. He soothed me with vague promises. We might be able to arrange something. There were admirably run homes for ex-nurses. It might be possible to obtain a place for Mother in one of them. Or some retired nurse might be willing to share the bungalow with her. When I had seen Mother fixed up satisfactorily, I could join him in Montreal and we could be married there.

Did he honestly believe that it would work out that way, or was he merely trying to let me down lightly? I had never known. A clean, sharp break would have been kinder in the long run than the ache of diminishing hope and the torment of misgivings which refused to be ignored.

For the first few months, there were letters to sustain me; glowing—for Cecil, normally so restrained—accounts of the Clinic and his grandfather's work. The one snag appeared to be that he wasn't the only descendant of the old man's who was following in his footsteps. There was a grand-daughter, too, who had been working with her grandfather ever since she had qualified. She was three years Cecil's senior—and didn't let him forget it.

"She reminds me vividly of Angela, with her bossiness," Cecil wrote. "Not in looks, though. To look at, she reminds me of your sister . . . 'La Belle Blonde', as Aylward used to call her."

Was his cousin beautiful as well as fair? I asked in my next letter.

"Very much so. Dazzlingly fair and quite lovely. Most unfair, with her indubitably brilliant brain . . ."

I can remember how my heart plummeted when I read that candid answer. I must have recognised it as the proverbial "writing on the wall". With a brilliant and beautiful cousin working with him and beside him, Cecil would have had to be a superman, or madly in love with me, not to have wavered in his allegiance.

I suppose it was fear, desperation, jealousy, and a frantic longing for reassurance which made me write to him challengingly: "Is there any point in our drifting on like this, with the Atlantic between us? Why don't you forget about me and marry your lovely, brilliant cousin? It would please your grandfather, wouldn't it? And settle the question of who will take over the Clinic when he retires."

Who was I to challenge Fate? I should have had less pride and more common-sense. I offered Cecil an "out". Could I blame him if he took it?

I was young then; too young and inexperienced and miserably frustrated to hold on grimly. I couldn't anticipate that within the next twelve months Mother would die . . . officially from bronchial pneumonia, but in actual fact because she had lost interest in life . . .

2

"And if thou wilt, remember,
And if thou wilt, forget."

C. G. ROSSETTI

"WHY don't you make something of your life?" Belle had demanded.

"What?" I asked myself again. I had had my chance of happiness, and I had thrown it away, through the very intensity of my love and longing. I had believed that Cecil must be aware of my desolation and desperation—and that he would respond.

Instead, he had written with obvious relief that, deeply though he felt my decision, he realised that it was "only sensible and only fair" that he should release me from "any commitment". He wished me everything that was good and would always remain my most sincere friend.

Belle had risen to change our plates. She brought back bowls of fresh fruit salad, with a jug of cream. The salad could have been delicious, but it had evidently been left in the coldest part of a very cold refrigerator for too long. It wasn't quite iced, but it struck icy cold to my tongue.

Helping herself to cream, she asked abruptly: "Do you ever hear from those Decanters nowadays?"

I started. I hadn't expected that question.

"They wrote when Mother died. You saw their letters," I said hurriedly. "I had a card from Angela, the following Christmas. Nothing since we gave up the bungalow."

"I wondered if your reluctance to go back to St. Cyriac's was because you were afraid of meeting Cecil again."

"Oh, no! Cecil . . ." I said confusedly. "Isn't he still in Montreal? With his grandfather?"

She shook her sleek fair head.

"He's in a practice in Sussex, not twenty miles from Netherfield Green. He visits St. Cyriac's on occasion, when he has patients there."

"Oh!" I said blankly. "Oh! How do you know?"

"I've kept in touch with the few friends I had there," she answered casually. "Also, by the merest chance, I met Angela not long ago. It was in Harrods. In her old 'queen to courtier' manner, she invited me to have a coffee with her. From curiosity, I accepted. She was looking older and rather strained. Not surprising. Her twin was the only person who mattered a damn to her."

"Her twin?" I echoed stupidly. "Aylward? Has anything happened to Aylward?"

"You don't know? You really have been living at the back of beyond," she said amusedly. "Admittedly, there wasn't much publicity. One imagines that it was deliberately played down. Pressure brought to bear, no doubt."

"About what? And by whom?" I nearly choked over a grape which felt like a lump of ice. "Don't be provoking, Belle, please! Tell me . . ."

"About Aylward? Or about Cecil?" She gave me a cool, probing stare. "Haven't you had any news of your erstwhile bosom friends since Cecil ran out on you?"

"He didn't. It was my own doing. I couldn't go on clinging . . ." I got out with an effort. "I thought his future lay in Canada; with his grandfather."

"You hadn't a hope—from the word 'go', you little idiot!" she said—as if stating the obvious. "Cecil never cared anything for you. His sole objective was to keep you and Aylward apart. Anyone could see that Aylward had a weakness for you, but he couldn't be allowed to indulge it, poor devil. I could have gone for that man, years ago, but I knew it was hopeless. He had to marry money. That was dinned into him good and hard by the rest of the family."

"Aylward's heiress? That was a joke," I said impatiently. "Cecil and I . . . Oh, there's no point in talking abut it now! You never had any time for the Decanters."

"You were blinkered by your emotions. I wasn't easily impressed by pretensions and I was furious at the way that family exploited you," Belle said coolly. "I knew you'd end by getting badly hurt . . . but what could I do? You persisted in glamorising those three."

35

"They were wonderful to me—and I loved them," I said defiantly. "Tell me Angela's news. What has Aylward been doing?"

"You haven't seen him since we left Netherfield Green?"

"No, except on TV. I used to watch his wildlife series until there was a fearful thunderstorm which wrecked Miss Henrietta's set. It was a very old set and she decided that it wasn't worth repairing. It needed a new transformer."

"You seem determined to make a martyr of yourself," Belle said derisively. "Stranded in the wilds without even a television set! If your old lady couldn't afford the repairs, I suppose she paid you the minimum and fed you on a starvation diet?"

In spite of her derisive tone, I glimpsed, to my surprise, a genuine concern in her ice-blue eyes.

"Miss Henrietta was on a diet, but the food was ample enough," I reassured her. "She treated me as a daughter. It wasn't anything like as tough a job as yours, Sister Theatre."

"Mine's full of interest and decidedly

36

rewarding. Like your friend Angela, I knew what I wanted—and I got it. Her studio is doing well, from her own account, and she's selling a certain amount of her work to the Press," Belle said dispassionately. "She escaped lightly from that ill-fated expedition—but Angela always did get away with things."

"What ill-fated expedition, Belle?"

"To make a documentary film about golden eagles in one of their natural habitats. A publicity stunt, financed by the frozen foods magnate, Harry Haylett. Golden Eagle is one of his brand names," Belle explained. "'Golden Eagle Foods bring you authentic recordings of golden eagles.' You know the kind of commercial that's popular these days."

I nodded.

"Just Aylward's thing. What went wrong?"

"Search me! Angela was cagey about the details. One of the party had a nasty fall, apparently. Aylward rushed to the rescue and took an even more disastrous tumble. By some misunderstanding, they'd got cut off from the rest of the expedition and weren't discovered till next morning."

"Aylward was badly injured?" I asked with a pang.

"Quite badly. He's recovering, though. Recently he was transferred to St. Cyriac's; presumably for his mother's convenience—or his fiancée's. The Decanters were always skilled hands at pulling strings," Belle said dryly.

"His fiancée?" I echoed.

"The Haylett girl. He did find his heiress eventually, but it hasn't done him much good. Poor devil!" Belle said again, with unusual feeling. "His mother and Angela never gave him a chance to be himself. All he wanted was a quiet country life. He hadn't any flair for the limelight, but they pushed him into it."

"I never guessed that you were interested in Aylward," I said wonderingly. "You concealed it remarkably well. I remember your caustic comments on 'Mr. Brawn' and how you liked to make him look small."

"Mainly to annoy Angela. I might have tried to annex him for the same reason, but I knew it would be a waste of time. You were the one he fancied, but, of course, that couldn't be allowed. The future Squire and the village blacksmith's daughter? That wasn't in the Decanters' book of words," she said ironically.

I stifled a sigh of exasperation. For a moment or two, I had felt a warming sense of kinship between us. I had almost believed that Belle had a genuine affection for me, and had suffered some qualms of remorse over her share in parting me from my love. I had even been tempted to tell her about Mary Decointre's advertisement.

Now, the old abyss had opened again between us. Her bitter prejudice against the Decanters was as strong as the cherished memories which bound me to them irrevocably. I hadn't wanted to go on loving Cecil, especially as I had supposed that he must have married his brilliant cousin long before this. There hadn't been many opportunities for romantic adventures in my secluded life with Miss Henrietta, but I'd had a mild, pleasantly undemanding thing going with the young partner of Miss Henrietta's middle-aged doctor. Had I been left 'the cottage'—which was actually a sizeable house—he might have come to the point. He was living in bachelor "digs"; over-priced even for these days.

He needed a wife and a home of his own, did young Dr. Alistair McCanning, but he was Scottish and shrewd, painstakingly "shopping around" before he committed himself. I had appreciated his company and cautious friendship. I had known that it wouldn't take much effort and encouragement on my part to convince him that we were a team. Instead, lacking any compelling incentive to secure him, I had helped him to keep our relationship on an even keel.

From a romantic viewpoint, I would have had more hope of Everton Gillard, Miss Henrietta's surprisingly trendy young solicitor, had he been within easy reach. On the half a dozen or so occasions when he had visited Miss Henrietta at her request, he had been charming to me—and not with a merely professional charm. On every visit, he had spent the evening and night with us. He had been as entertaining a companion at breakfast as at supper—which spoke well for his self-control or for his interest in me. The spare room was just an attic under the eaves, with an irregular, sloping ceiling, on which a man as tall as Everton was guaranteed to bump his head, and a disgracefully lumpy old mattress and camp bed, acquired by Miss Henrietta at a jumble sale. The little room was hot and airless in summer and ice cold in winter. Most young men would have been decidedly disgruntled after a night in it.

"Wool-gathering?" Belle asked sharply. "You've what Aylward Decanter used to call your 'secret garden' look."

"You seem to remember a lot about Aylward," I said significantly.

"Why not? He was always pleasant enough to me. It was the other two I couldn't stand." She gave me another probing glance. "It makes me see red to know that you're still hankering after that spoilt, selfish, self-seeking Cecil."

3

"Only a memory of the same . . ."
R. BROWNING

BELLE would think I was crazy, I reflected, as I wriggled into a more comfortable position on the red plush settee in the corridor. Had it been the knowledge of my own folly, or a vague feeling of guilt towards my sister which had made it impossible for me to tell her about my appointment with Mary Decointre? I could remember clearly that same obscure sense of guilt which had haunted me in the old days, when I had been riding off to the Hall, leaving Belle at home.

As a child, I had reasoned desperately: "Belle doesn't want me. Belle doesn't care a scrap about me. They care. I matter to them . . ."

I had been at fault on both counts. Belle had cared. In her own restrained fashion, she had been and still was concerned about

42

me. The Decanters, who had appeared to regard me as "one of the family", had forgotten all about me. Had I no proper pride, that I hadn't been able to resist the impulse to answer Mary Decointre's advertisement for a "nurse companion, able to drive, and fond of country life"?

I didn't have to sit here, outside Mary Decointre's suite, awaiting my turn for an interview. I had answered her advertisement on Miss Henrietta's typewriter and signed my application merely "C. Smith". I could fade out now without seeing Mary Decointre; without subjecting myself—or her—to the possible embarrassment of an encounter.

Yes, but then I should be left with only those snippets of news from Belle. I shouldn't know what had happened between Cecil and his brilliant cousin to bring him back to England. I shouldn't know how badly Aylward had been hurt, or whether his heiress was still ready to marry him. I shouldn't know what had gone wrong with Mary Decointre and why she needed a nurse. I couldn't trail back to Cornwall with so many questions unanswered.

Music was drifting out from behind one of the closed doors I was facing. A radio? Or a record player? I recognised one of the latest songs to make the charts, set in a minor key, with a slow, heavy beat.

"There's always one who
    remembers . . .
One who remembers . . .
One who remembers . . .
And one who forgets."

The words of the refrain sounded like the echo of my own thoughts. "One who remembers . . ."? Why did I have to be the one who remembered? Why couldn't I forget the calm, decisive, possessive fashion in which, all those years ago, Cecil had said: "You're going to marry me . . . That's a promise . . ."? Why couldn't I forget the gleam in his eyes and the way in which his thin, clever face had lit up whenever he had talked of his plans for the future; our future? Why couldn't I forget the warm clasp of his hands and the pressure of his lips when we had parted?

The nearest door opened and shut again with a sharp click, which was almost a slam. A girl in nurse's uniform paused beside me. She looked young to be an SRN. She had untidy fairish hair, a childishly rounded face, hotly flushed, and a youthfully plump figure.

"You can go in now," she informed me. Tossing back her mane like a restive pony, she added: "You're more than welcome to the job. Nothing was said about a mental case. That's not my line at all."

"Mental case?" I echoed blankly.

"Well, call her highly strung and neurotic, if you want to put a gloss on it. 'A traumatic shock', was what she said. The mamma bird, I mean. I'd say the girl's half-way round the bend and liable to be more than a handful," she snorted. "Honest, I could have slapped her. One of those filthy rich little beasts, with doting parents, is my guess."

"Girl? What girl?" I began, bewildered, but, with another snort and toss of her mane, she was cantering down the corridor to the lifts.

I got up, stretching my cramped limbs. I wasn't in uniform. I had rarely worn

45

uniform while I had been with Miss Henrietta.

"No need to advertise the fact that I'm on my last lap," she had said, with that humour and courage which I had found so endearing. "I plan to keep my end up and live a comparatively normal life as long as is humanly possible. I shall introduce you to casual visitors as my young niece. Any objection?"

I had answered that I would much prefer it to be that way. I hadn't sat for my finals, thanks to Mother's collapse, so, in uniform, I was apt to feel something of a fraud. In Cornwall, Miss Henrietta and I had usually gone around in sweaters and slacks. For this trip, I was wearing a dark green and black striped suit, not new but well-cut. The green brought out the deep green of my eyes . . . "the colour of horse-chestnut leaves", as Aylward had observed at our first encounter.

The combination of those eyes and my horse-chestnut red hair was fairly memorable. I couldn't hope that Mary Decointre would fail to recognise me.

The "Come in, please!" which answered my tap was unmistakably in Mary

Decointre's voice. She had been Canadian born and bred, and she had never shed her Western drawl. In fact, the three young Decanters had had it, too, when I'd first known them. In subsequent years, Angela had deliberately eliminated her trace of an accent and Cecil's had worn off in his early teens. In his television programmes, Aylward still looked and sounded like the hero of a Western. To me, that suggestion of the "wide open spaces" remained part of his charm. I thought it must give viewers a sense of anticipation—as if at any moment he would spring into the saddle or reach for his revolver. Miss Henrietta had agreed with me.

"He has that indescribable Something— star quality—personality . . . character . . . that makes a man stand out in a crowd," she had pronounced. "Any girl would get a kick from being swept up into his saddle."

Aylward's drawl would always hold a nostalgic quality for me. So, I realised now, would his mother's. She came forward to meet me, hand outstretched . . . and the intervening years seemed to vanish.

Mary Decointre had scarcely changed at all. Her dark hair was a little greyer, her attractive, expressive face more lined, and her slight, wiry figure thinner, but I found it difficult to believe that I hadn't seen her for over five years. Even the firm, warm clasp of her lean but surprisingly strong fingers was exactly as I'd remembered it.

"So good of you to call," she said, and glanced down at my letter, which she was clutching in her left hand. "Miss Smith, isn't it? Miss C. Smith?"

Then, she looked directly at me, and her fine, greyish blue eyes widened in astonishment.

"Why, it's Constant! Little Conker, as the boys used to call you. My dear, this is a surprise! A very pleasant surprise . . . especially after some of the nurses I've interviewed. But . . . surely, you're not taking private cases? Sit down and tell me all about yourself."

She caught my hand in hers again, and drew me down beside her, on to a small settee, which was facing an electric fire. The room was furnished in the usual adequate but impersonal style that one would expect in a moderately priced hotel, but already Mary Decointre had stamped it with something of her lively, restless vitality.

A mackintosh, a scarf, a pair of leather gloves, a sheaf of magazines and an opened newspaper were strewn around, and a pair of walking shoes lay on their sides half under the settee. A tea-tray with two used cups, and an ash-tray piled high with stubs stood on the table, flanked by a water jug crammed full of long-stemmed, colourful tulips. On her side of the settee was a little pile of crumpled-looking letters. She put my letter down on top of the pile.

"Oh, it is good to see you again, though really I guess I should be furious with you!" she said, with a characteristic jerk of her beautifully shaped head. "You caused my poor Cecil a lot of heart-ache. I know how you felt about your mother, but your sister was equally responsible for her. Poor Linda! I missed her badly, after Belle had whisked you both off to Devon. I hope she didn't suffer?"

We talked for a minute or two about my mother. Then Mary Decointre sighed.

"It is tough to be left without your man, when you're still comparatively young and active. Most of us manage to carry on, though, for the sake of our families. If Linda had had a son, I doubt if she would have given up so easily," she said candidly. "Belle never needed anything from her mother . . . and you had us. Linda used to accuse me—playfully, of course—of having taken you over to make my family complete. We'd planned to have two sons and two daughters."

"I used to feel as though I belonged to you," I admitted.

"So did we. That's why we were all rather hurt at the 'vanishing act' you staged after Linda's death."

"Vanishing act?" I echoed perplexedly. "I didn't vanish. We gave up the bungalow we'd rented for Mother, because Belle preferred to take a flat nearer the hospital. I found a job in Cornwall, and I've been there ever since."

"We wrote to you—at the bungalow—and our letters came back with 'Address unknown' on them. Then we wrote 'care of' your sister, and those letters were ignored."

"I didn't have them. I didn't hear again

from any of you, after your letters of sympathy."

There was a brief, uneasy silence between us. I thought, with rising indignation, that Belle must have deliberately suppressed those letters. They must have reached her. Oh, how could she have kept them from me? She must have known that I was yearning to get in touch with the Decanters, but that pride would prevent me from making the first move.

"How very odd," Mary Decointre said at last, a pucker between her dark, arched brows. "That didn't occur to us. We thought that you were probably engaged or married . . . and loth to tell us about it."

"No," I said flatly. "I was looking after a semi-invalid. I didn't feel like going back to hospital."

She nodded, as if she understood . . . and there was another awkward silence. Glancing at her again, I could see that she had aged more than had been apparent at first sight. When she wasn't smiling, her features had a drawn, strained look, and her slender shoulders were sagging.

"You've been ill?" I said tentatively. "You need nursing?"

She shook her head impatiently.

"Not ill. Just worried—and run down —or so our doctor says. You remember Dr. Coburn-MacDonald? He insisted that I must hire skilled help, if I wasn't to run the risk of a collapse."

"Help?" I repeated inquiringly.

"With Katy. She's a grave responsibility, and I've had no experience of spoilt, nervy, problem children."

She rose with one of her old, swift, restless movements, and crossed to a small sideboard.

"Let's have a drink," she said, over her shoulder. "Scotch all right for you?"

"Very weak, then, please. I'm driving."

Her hands were shaking, I noted apprehensively, as she splashed whisky into two tumblers. As if conscious of my scrutiny, she said wryly: "I'm drinking and smoking far too much these days. The result of strain. If only that wretched girl hadn't quarrelled with her father and landed herself on me . . ."

"What girl?"

"Katy Haylett. My daughter-in-law to

be. At least, she was. Now . . . I don't know . . . and neither does she."

She handed me my drink and sat down beside me, one finger tapping restively against her own glass.

"It seemed such a grand break for Aylward . . . only daughter and heiress of Harry Haylett, the Seafood King, sweetly pretty and quite crazy about the boy," she went on jerkily. "It did cross my mind that she was rather young and fragile for him, and not fearfully bright, but, as Angela said, with all that money behind her, Katy didn't need to be a brain . . . and no one could call Aylward an intellectual."

I remembered what Belle had hinted, about the pressure his mother and sister had exerted upon Aylward. Had they manoeuvred him into this engagement? But . . . he wasn't a boy now, to be pushed around by his womenfolk.

I said impulsively: "Not an intellectual, perhaps, but he knows a lot about natural history, and he has the knack of arousing enthusiasm in his viewers."

"His programmes have been handicapped by lack of funds. With Harry

Haylett's backing, he ought to have been able to make some first-class documentaries. If only Katy hadn't insisted on going with the expedition . . ." Her brows furrowed. "Silly, wilful young thing! I've no doubt in my own mind that she was responsible for the accident."

"What does Aylward say about it?"

"Nothing. That's what's so upsetting. He had severe concussion, and it left him with partial amnesia. He can't remember anything about the expedition . . ."

"Oh? Probably only temporary," I said, wondering why she sounded so concerned. "It often happens that way . . . a temporary black-out."

"I know that—and there's no need to make a tragedy out of it—but you young people are so impatient," she said edgily. "You can't wait for anything, can you?"

"I can't?" I said, bewildered, and remembering with a pang just how long I had waited for Cecil.

"I don't mean you, my child. Your age group," she said, and jerked her head towards an inner door. "Hear that?"

It was the record player again, with the same record.

"Katy's theme song. 'One who remembers . . .' It's getting on my nerves. She plays it over and over again," she said wryly.

"Katy? She's here?"

"Didn't I explain? That's why I'm looking for a nurse. The child clings to me, but I can't cope with her."

"Is she ill?"

"She did have a mild attack of pneumonia as a result of the shock and exposure, but now the trouble is emotional. She has nightmares and crying fits." Mary pushed the greying hair back from her puckered forehead in a distracted gesture. "Cecil says she's had a traumatic shock and needs careful handling. I think she's behaving like a spoilt baby. Her father had to go out to the West Indies on a business trip and wanted to take her with him for her convalescence. Would she go? Oh, no! She wanted to stay near Aylward."

"I can understand that."

"If she'd had Aylward's interests at heart, she would have humoured her father, instead of quarrelling with him and working herself into this state," Mary said

55

ruefully. "Every time we visit Aylward, she comes away in the depths of depression . . . and I'm terrified that she'll do herself some serious damage."

So that was what the plump young nurse had meant when she had spoken of "a mental case"?

"I'm so sorry. Do you think I could help?" I asked.

"It would be a great relief if you were game to try," she answered unhesitatingly. "Katy's father is paying, so you can name your own terms, but it will need patience, and unremitting watchfulness."

"Some serious damage . . ." "Unremitting watchfulness . . ." The two phrases she had used clicked into place, and I realised belatedly why Mary Decointre had that strained look.

"You have suicide in mind?" I challenged her. "But . . . if she's crazy about Aylward and he's recovering, that doesn't make sense."

"We don't know yet how complete his recovery will be. There may be permanent lameness. That's on the child's mind," she said wearily. "What she finds most

56

distressing, of course, is his inability to remember *her*."

"Oh!" I caught my breath, startled. "He has forgotten her? His fiancée?"

She nodded sombrely.

"Katy—her father—the expedition— and virtually everything that's happened in the past year or so. Katy takes it very much to heart."

"No wonder you're looking tired and strained!" I said compassionately, "It must have been grim for you. Please let me try to shift some of the load off your shoulders."

"I'll be thankful to, if the child agrees. The final decision has to be hers—and she's not easily satisfied. She has faulted every applicant so far . . . too young, too old, too bossy, too dull, too cold and hard . . . too painfully hearty . . ."

4

*"With women the heart argues, not
the mind."*

I HAD inherited the "Katy" books
from my father's mother, who had
kept all the books she had treasured
in her childhood. I had been a rapid and
omnivorous reader ever since I had learnt
to read. The Katy of *What Katy Did* had
been a very real person to me, and so the
name possessed deep-rooted associations in
my mind.

Nothing could have been much more
unlike my mental picture of a "Katy" than
the girl who lay sprawled out on the
double bed like a discarded doll. She
lacked the rounded, rosy cheeks of an
expensive doll, though she had a fairy
doll's long flaxen hair and wide, forget-
me-not blue eyes.

Fair, fragile and flower-like were the
adjectives which came first to my mind.

58

Her skin had the pale, matt texture of some flower petals and she looked as if a rough grasp would leave her bruised and wilting. Her long, fair hair lay around her shoulders in a dishevelled mass. There were traces of tears on her cheeks, and dark shadows under her eyes. A romantic might have described her as "looking pathetically small and lost in that big bed". I didn't, even in my first hurried scrutiny, see her as pathetic. Sickly looking, yes, and overstrung, but not "pathetic". She had, I noticed, taken care to pull the plump blue eiderdown over her, and there was an open box of peppermint creams on the table beside her, with the exposed layer half finished. Did girls who were contemplating suicide cover their limbs carefully from stray draughts and munch peppermint creams? I wouldn't have thought so. Admittedly, my experience of neurotic patients was severely limited, but I couldn't associate peppermint creams with a haunting remorse and despair. They were, to me, one of the most appetising, comforting and normal forms of con-fectionery.

Mary Decointre, having murmured brief introductions, had retreated back to the sitting-room. She had closed the communicating door after her but, as if it had been made of glass, I fancied I could see her at the sideboard, refilling her glass.

Katy had said: "How d'you do?" in a limp voice and then relapsed into silence. She was eyeing me warily from behind a screen of artificially darkened, drooping eyelashes. She must still be in her teens, I thought. I didn't intend to be stared out of countenance by a girl so much my junior. Unbidden, I sat down on the end of her bed and returned her scrutiny coolly. "Silence can be a weapon as well as a shield." That had been one of Miss Henrietta's dictums and it had lodged in my mind. I was here to be interviewed, not to interview, and I wasn't going to be stampeded into speech.

I settled back comfortably and tried to sum Katy Haylett up, as Miss Henrietta would have done when introducing a new character into a novel. Dressed and groomed for an occasion, with some incentive to sparkle, Katy could have passed as a "lovely", I decided. She hadn't the incisively chiselled features which gave Belle her classic beauty. I couldn't imagine that any man would nickname Katy Haylett "La Belle Blonde". Katy's nose was short and mildly retroussé. She had a short upper lip, too, over-small uneven teeth which were slightly protruding, an indecisive lower lip, and a pointed chin.

"Well?" she demanded fretfully. "Haven't you anything to say for yourself?"

"Plenty. Sorry! I was thinking," I answered.

"What were you thinking? You were staring at me," she said suspiciously.

"I was thinking that it didn't suit you to look woebegone," I told her truthfully. "You're more the gamine than the fading lily type, aren't you?"

"Woebegone?" she echoed, as if the word were strange to her. She wrinkled her nose distastefully. "Woebegone? It sounds horrid ... and madly old-fashioned."

"Yes. I suppose it is old-fashioned," I conceded. "It goes with 'eyelashes aquiver with tear-drops, like morning dew, and eyes like drowned forget-me-nots', and the kind of heroine who can look heart-appealing when she weeps, instead of getting a reddened nose and a blotched skin like most of us . . ."

"What on earth are you talking about? What heroine? Are you making fun of me?"

There was childish resentment in her tone. I remembered that Mary had observed that Katy wasn't over-bright.

"Sorry!" I said swiftly. "I've just been looking after a novelist. I acted as her secretary, and I got interested in her way of seeing and describing her characters."

"A novelist? A well-known writer?"

"Quite well known—at least, to judge from her sales. Henrietta Pearson."

"I've read some of her books. They were good. I don't like grim stories. Why aren't you still with her?"

"She died."

"Oh? Why?"

"She was elderly—well over eighty—and had a heart condition."

"Did you mind? Does it upset you? When people die, I mean?"

"Naturally, I'm sorry. The exact degree of grief depends on the circumstances.

Death isn't always a tragedy. Sometimes it's a release . . . an open gateway."

"It terrifies me. I nearly died, you know. Did Mrs. Decointre tell you?"

"Only that you had been involved in a nasty accident and had had pneumonia . . ."

"It was a nightmare. A ghastly nightmare. I can't get over it. I shall never get over it," she cried out huskily, lips quivering. "I can't sleep without dreaming about it. That sudden jolt and then falling through space and feeling as if all my bones were broken . . . and then that endless night, when I didn't dare to move and didn't know whether Aylward was alive or dead. Nobody can imagine what it was like . . ."

"It must have been grim. A shattering experience . . ." Especially, I thought, to a spoilt darling who had perhaps never encountered severe discomfort let alone pain and terror before. "The horror will fade in time. You won't forget, but it will become less vivid."

"Well, that's a different one!" The blue eyes opened more widely and seemed to be considering me appraisingly. "Everyone

63

else has said: 'Don't think about it. Forget it. It's all over now.' Only, it isn't over for me. Can you understand that?"

"Perfectly. Because I'm not good at forgetting, either." Involuntarily, I glanced at the opulent-looking portable record player which was flanking the peppermint creams. "I'm afraid I'm one of those who remembers. I've a painfully acute, photographic memory."

"Oh? And are there things you long to forget?"

"Quite a number of them. I try not to let them haunt me, but every now and then someone or something flicks a switch, and it's as if I'm compelled to watch a film of the past, unrolling before my eyes."

I hadn't told anyone that, except Cecil, years ago, and he had found it difficult to grasp my meaning. I certainly hadn't intended to speak of it to this stranger. The words had been drawn out of me—as if by her desperate need.

She was the type who would naturally dramatise and exaggerate her symptoms. That I had recognised instantly. I had also recognised genuine terror and something not far from despair.

"*Oh!*" she said again, and a trace of colour crept into her waxen skin. "Oh, yes! It is like that. You do understand . . . you really do. It is like a film, only some of the scenes are blurred. I can see a hand . . . reaching out to push me . . . but I can't see whose it is." She paused, one hand pressing against her lips in a childish gesture. Her blue eyes searched my face. Then she went on defiantly: "They'll tell you that's nonsense . . . that I slipped and am suffering from a guilt complex, so I have to blame somebody else. It isn't true. There was this sharp jolt in the small of my back. I can feel it now. You must believe me."

I nodded slowly. The thought crossed my mind that, if someone had given her a sharp shove in the back, Katy couldn't have seen the hand in question. That part of the play-back must have been added by her imagination. I didn't voice that conclusion, though. I didn't want to check her confidences.

I had come into the room acutely sorry for Mary Decointre and eager to carry some of her load for her. Now, I was perceiving that Katy's need for help was equally urgent and probably less easily met. The kind of brisk, practical nurse who would counsel her: "Forget it. Don't think about it . . ." would merely drive her in on herself to brood until she was lost in a welter of fears and suspicions.

My compassion was for Katy now. Nothing in her past life could have conditioned her to face the stress and torment of violent and devastating emotions. I wasn't "a born nurse", as Mother had said Belle was, but I had inherited a flair for following the workings of people's minds. I fancied I had inherited it from Father. Mother had been chiefly concerned with bodily ills. It had been Father who had looked beneath the surface and seen what made people tick.

I could feel Katy's reaching out for me; clutching at me as if at a life-line, though she had scarcely moved. Some part of me was shrinking away from the contact, belatedly recalling Belle's warnings, and urging me: "Don't get involved with this child and the Decanters. You'll only be hurt all over again . . . Forget them . . ."

The other, stronger part was insisting: "You'll never forget, so why waste any more time in trying? This child is in desperate need of help—and you owe the Decanters something. Whatever went wrong between you and Cecil, Aylward wasn't to blame. Aylward always treated you kindly and chivalrously. It won't hurt you to lend his sweetheart a helping hand . . . or, if it does hurt, who's afraid of a little pain?"

"Why don't you answer? Do you believe me?" Katy demanded. "Perhaps they've told you that I'm a nut-case?"

I shook my head.

"Certainly not. Is there any reason why I shouldn't believe you? You should know whether your foot slipped or not."

"I slipped—but only after I'd felt that jarring pain in the back. That's what caught me off balance. So . . . I don't have to feel guilty, do I? I couldn't help falling."

There was something feverish in her tone and in the sudden glitter of her blue eyes. Her forehead looked as if it would be clammy to the touch. I wondered uneasily if Katy was running a temperature.

"An accident is just that. Something for

which nobody is directly responsible," I answered slowly. "It's futile to dwell on 'if onlys', though most of us do. I saw my father killed . . . by an accident. A horse lashed out as he was bending to shoe it, and caught him on the temple. I kept on thinking afterwards: 'If only I'd been holding that horse, he wouldn't have reared up suddenly. If only I'd been watching, I could have cried out a warning. Or, if I hadn't been there, talking to her, Angela might have been concentrating on the horse . . .'"

"Angela?" she echoed. "Angela Decointre?"

"Yes. It was her horse. My father ran The Forge at Netherfield Green, years ago."

"So that was what Mrs. Decointre meant when she said: 'This is Miss Smith. She's quite an old family friend . . .'? You're a friend of Angela's? And of Aylward's?"

"I was, when we were children. I haven't seen Angela or Aylward or—or Cecil, for over five years. It was just by chance that I spotted Mrs. Decointre's advertisement."

"Then . . . could I trust you not to gang up with them against me?"

"Of course. Why should they 'gang up' against you, anyway? Aren't you engaged to Aylward?" I said perplexedly.

"I was . . ." The feverish intensity of her gaze was suddenly blurred by tears; tears which brimmed over and splashed down her cheeks. "It—it was wonderful. I was never so happy before. I just adored him. He was such marvellous fun. Now . . . he doesn't even recognise me . . . and he looks dreadful. . ."

"Don't cry," I said automatically. "Tears don't really help. I don't even find them a relief, because I always get a headache after I've been howling. Besides, you haven't any need to weep over Aylward. He isn't dead and he hasn't gone off with some other girl. This amnesia is a temporary thing, and one can bear anything if one is sure it won't last."

She blinked and reached for a sodden wisp of handkerchief. She rubbed it across her eyes. Then she gave me a watery smile.

"I like you. You're different," she said naïvely. "Not like a nurse at all. More

69

human, somehow. Will you stay with me? And not be furious if I wake you in the night by screaming? And not force sleeping pills down me? They only make the nightmares worse."

"Yes," I said. "I can imagine that they would. They don't suit me, either. They give me bad dreams. I know, because I did try taking them for a time, when I couldn't sleep. In the end, I realised that I would rather lie awake."

"Oh, so would I! You do understand," she said in a tone of heart-felt relief. "Can you stay here tonight? You can have Mrs. Decointre's room next door and she can move into another. She won't mind. She'll be relieved. She doesn't like me very much. Her patience is fraying and I'm driving her to drink."

That was said so naïvely and earnestly that involuntarily I laughed. For a moment, Katy glowered at me. Then, suddenly, she gave a weak giggle.

"It does sound funny . . . but it's true. She keeps on swigging whisky, and I know it's my fault. I get on her nerves," she confessed. "She'd love to slap me—and I almost wish she would. It's horrid to feel you're being humoured and put up with just because you've a lot of money."

"Yes. It must be. Only, you haven't lots of money, surely? You mean that your father has."

"Oh, Father's what people call 'stinking rich'! I'm not, but I do have some money of my own. It came from my mother. She put up the capital to give Father his start, but he paid her back in the end, and she left the money to me. I wanted to invest it in Aylward's films, but he wouldn't let me. I was cross at the time, but I respected him for feeling that way," she said seriously. "He didn't mind letting Father stake him to the 'Eagle' films—because that was purely a business deal. Only now, of course, he's lost the chance . . . all through me. I do feel grim about it."

"Naturally," I agreed. "I'd like to hear all about the project later. Now, if you want me to stay, I'd better tell Mrs. Decointre so, and fetch my luggage."

"She can come in here. You're not to make plans with her behind my back," Katy said, suddenly imperious. "I'm not sure that I trust her . . . and I certainly don't trust Angela. They don't really want Aylward to marry me."

"That's no affair of mine," I said firmly. "But, if you can't trust me to do my best for you, I would prefer you to find someone else. I've never been accused yet of being disloyal to a patient, and I should take a dim view of it."

"You've a temper," she said—as if in surprise. "Well, I suppose you would have, with that reddish hair. Only, don't be angry with *me* . . . please. I didn't mean to upset you. I simply have to be sure that you're on my side."

"Nurses don't take sides, but naturally a patient's interests come first . . ."

Later, I was to reflect ruefully upon how smug I must have sounded to that frightened, heart-sick child. At the time, I honestly couldn't see that I was likely to be involved in "taking sides", or tempted to be anything but loyal to my patient. It's easy to believe in one's own integrity and impartiality when neither has been seriously tested.

Perhaps if I could have foreseen what lay ahead, I shouldn't have altered course. Fear was an emotion I had rarely experienced. I hadn't had any reason to learn how to duck away from danger. I hadn't even learnt to recognise its scent.

"As long as you remember that and put me first . . ." Katy wrinkled her nose again. "Oh, blast! That sounds horrid. Like a typical spoilt brat. I didn't mean it that way. It's simply that, with Father in the West Indies—and livid with me, anyway—I haven't anyone to back me up or give me a hand."

"Point taken," I said. "Hang on to me as hard as you please. I'm pretty steady on my feet."

"Then, will £70 a week and all expenses suit you?" she asked.

"Seventy per week? That's far too much. I'm not an SRN. I never sat for my finals," I protested.

"It's what Daddy suggested. He paid a month's money into my account before he left. At least, actually, he paid in £500, to cover a nurse's salary and expenses," she explained. "He said £70 would be about right, and should give me a fair selection. 'If you want the best, show that you're prepared to pay for it.' That's his motto. 'Don't go to the bargain counter and then complain if what you bought is coming apart at the seams', is another saying of his. So you needn't worry about costing too much."

"You don't buy people as if they were garments in a sale," I said, divided between amusement and exasperation. "I hope I shan't 'come apart at the seams', but, as I've warned you, I'm not fully qualified. Your father might think I was dear at the price."

"Oh, no! He'd go for you," she said confidently. "He'd say you were 'good value'. That's another of his pet phrases."

The door to the sitting-room swung open and Mary Decointre paused in the doorway, glancing from me to Katy.

"I don't want to hurry you, my dear, but there is another nurse waiting for her interview," she announced.

"Send her away! This one will do," Katy said impatiently. "Miss Smith, is it? How prim that sounds! It doesn't suit you at all! What's your Christian name?"

"Constant. Constant, with a 't', not a 'c'."

"Constant Smith? That sounds like a

Pilgrim Father or something equally dire. Haven't you a pet name?"

"My sister calls me 'Connie', but Aylward—Aylward Decointre—nick-named me 'Conker' years ago. After the conker trees which grew around The Forge."

"What on earth is a conker tree?" Katy asked blankly.

"Didn't you ever collect conkers as a kid? Horse-chestnuts," I explained.

"I was never a village child," Katy protested, with naïve snobbery. "I've always lived in London, and I went to private schools. I don't know much about trees. Was your father really a village blacksmith?"

"*The* village blacksmith. The only one for many miles," Mary Decointre contrib-uted. "A delightful man. Angela fell madly in love with him when we first came to the Hall."

"Angela did?" I said incredulously. "I never guessed that."

"Naturally not. You were too young. Your sister suspected it—and strongly disapproved." Mary paused, her forehead furrowing again. "You are sure about this,

Constant? Sure you would like to tackle the job?"

"Why not?" I asked, slightly chilled by her question. I had supposed that she would be relieved that I appeared to have taken Katy's capricious fancy.

"Working for friends can lead to complications. Did I tell you that we hope to have Aylward home again quite soon? He'll probably need a certain amount of nursing. You won't mind lending a hand with him?"

"Of course not. I'll be glad to help."

The warning had been clear enough in her troubled tone and glance, but I shrugged it off impatiently.

5

*"This heat of hope, or cold of fear
My foolish heart could never
   bear."*

SIR JOHN SNELLING

IN spite of the unfamiliar bed, and the over-elaborate dinner, which had been in such marked contrast to the light suppers I had shared with Miss Henrietta, I must have fallen asleep a minute or two after I had switched off the light. I was deeply and dreamlessly asleep when I was jerked back to consciousness by frantic screams.

There was a startled moment, as I heaved myself up on one elbow, when I supposed dazedly that I must have woken from a nightmare. Then I realised that the sounds echoing in my ears were actual, not imaginary. Automatically, I swung myself clear of the bedclothes. It was when I reached for the bedside lamp's switch and failed to find it that I remembered where I was—and with whom.

I called: "I'm coming—" and fumbled in the darkness for my dressing-gown and slippers. The communicating door, between Katy's room and the bedroom Mary Decointre had hastily vacated, had been left wide open, at Katy's request. I groped my way to the doorway and found the switch just inside Katy's room. In the sudden brightness, I blinked across at the bed. Most of the bedclothes were trailing on to the floor. Katy was half crouching, half sprawling, her fair hair veiling her face, both hands clutching at the bedclothes. She was calling out, but the words were muffled and incoherent.

I went over to her and put one hand lightly on her heaving shoulders. She gave a violent jerk and screamed again.

"Katy! Wake up!" I said, giving her a slight shake. "You're dreaming. Katy—"

She moaned out: "No . . . Oh, no! Don't! Please . . ." then shuddered convulsively.

"Katy!" I said again, urgently. "Snap out of it!"

She gave a startled gasp, shook back her curtain of hair, and blinked at me.

"Oh! Oh, it's *you* . . ." she said, in obvious relief. "What's happened? Was I dreaming again?"

"Apparently. Don't you remember?"

She shuddered again, and clutched at me. I sat down on the bed and she hid her face against my shoulder. Her hair, brushing my chin and neck, had a young, clean fragrance, reminiscent of hayfields. There was a young feel about her quivering body, too. Her limbs might have been a puppy's.

I said: "It's over now. Just relax . . ." and then, impulsively, I asked: "How old are you, Katy?"

"Eighteen. Old enough to make a Will. And I did . . . make mine . . . before we left London . . ." she answered jerkily. "Foolish of me . . . wasn't it? Sticking my neck out . . . as Angela would say. Asking for a jab in the back . . ."

"You're talking nonsense," I said uneasily.

"Daddy wanted me to wait . . . till I was married. He said it was putting temptation in Aylward's way . . . and humiliating myself, too," she got out, in a muffled voice. "He said nobody ought to need bribing to marry me. Cecil said that, too."

"Cecil . . ." My limbs jerked as if at a sudden tug at my heart-strings. "You discussed your Will with Cecil?"

"With all of them. Why not? I thought they were like my own family. Cecil was very nice to me . . . like an elder brother," she answered defiantly. "Why should I have had any secrets from them?"

"You poor child . . ."

That was what I had believed, too, for years and years. I had been certain that I was accepted as "one of the family". It had been sheer illusion. It must have been, or why had all the Decanters drifted away, out of touch?

"They're so much a family . . . and I've always longed to be one of a family," Katy murmured. "I thought they really cared about me . . . apart altogether from the money . . ."

"I thought that, too . . . years ago."

"Did you?" She raised her head and looked at me challengingly. "Were you in love with Aylward, when you were a girl?"

When I was a girl? She made it sound like a century ago. Perhaps to Katy, still in her teens, anyone on the wrong side of twenty-five did appear to belong to another generation. But . . . if that were so, the Decanters were on my side of the age gap. The twins would be thirty next year.

"No," I answered. "I didn't dare. I hero-worshipped him, naturally, but I didn't see myself as Cinderella. Besides, all along, Angela insisted that he would have to marry money—if he wanted to keep the Hall."

"*Don't*! If—if I'd been killed, he would have had the money—and he wouldn't have had to marry me. How can I forget that?"

"If he loves you . . ." Aware of the rising note of panic in her voice, I kicked myself mentally for having been led into this discussion. As her nurse, it was my job to soothe her. "You must know whether he loves you or not. At least, one is supposed to know . . ."

"Is one? How?" she demanded bleakly.

How, indeed? Had I known? I could have sworn that I meant nearly as much to Cecil as he had meant to me . . . and yet hadn't he snatched at his freedom when I had offered it?

"I never thought Aylward cared about money—or very deeply about the Hall."

"Well, he can't care much about *me*, or he wouldn't have forgotten me. That's what Cecil says. Cecil believes that people forget what they're secretly yearning to forget . . ."

"I've heard that theory. In this instance, it can't be true. Aylward wouldn't have chosen to forget all about the expedition," I reasoned.

"N-no. That's something." She sighed. "Oh, I couldn't bear it if I lost him! I should curl up and die."

Had I felt like that? If I had, pride had prevented me from admitting it. I had tried to shrug my shoulders and tell myself that, if Cecil married his brilliant and beautiful cousin, he would regret it eventually. He could never share with her all the memories which had held us together. Perhaps I hadn't believed that he could forget me . . .

"One doesn't, you know. Curl up and die, I mean. One plods on, hoping," I began.

"For *what?*" She shivered. "It's the feeling that someone hates me, and is working against me, which frightens me. Who is it? Who pushed me?"

"Are you sure someone did?"

I hadn't taken that assertion seriously. I had thought it was a childish excuse for having brought disaster on the expedition. A small child will complain tearfully that "the nasty table bumped my head". I had supposed Katy's "somebody pushed me" to come into the same category.

"Of course I'm sure," she said crossly. "I felt it, didn't I? That sudden blow in the back . . ."

"Perhaps something fell on you. If anyone had been close enough to push you, surely you would have known who it was?"

Her only answer was another shivering fit. She wasn't putting on an act. She really was frightened. Chilled, too, physically and emotionally.

"You need a hot-water bottle and a hot drink," I said.

"At past three in the morning?" She indicated the travelling clock on the dressing-table. "There wouldn't be anyone on duty now."

"I've a tiny picnic stove and kettle. No milk or tea, but I expect there's fruit juice in the sitting-room."

"Don't leave me. Don't go away," she pleaded, as if she were eight rather than eighteen, and afraid of the dark. "If I doze off, the nightmare will grab me again."

"Not to worry! I'll just get the stove."

I released myself from her clammy, clutching hands, glad that I'd had the foresight to bring my picnic case with me. Not that I had foreseen the need for it at three a.m. I had stowed it in the car as an economy measure. On a long drive, to have picnic snacks was considerably cheaper than to stop at hotels or restaurants. I was obliged to count my pennies. I hadn't been able to earn anything in the years I'd spent looking after Mother. The few hundreds Belle and I had inherited on Mother's death were still invested in a Building Society.

"Leave the capital there, as an emergency fund, and just take the interest," Belle had advised me, and I had agreed.

As Belle had guessed, the salary paid me

by Miss Henrietta—when she'd remembered it—hadn't amounted to union rates. To have money to spare for riding, still my favourite leisure time pursuit, I'd had to economise where I could.

Katy sat up, hands clasped round her knees, watching me through her curtain of hair as I set up the little stove and put the kettle on to boil. I could feel her gaze following me when I went through into the sitting-room for fruit juice and glasses. On an impulse, I laced one drink with whisky, in the hope that it might help Katy to sleep.

"You're efficient," she said, when she had her hot drink and hot-water bottle. "Yet you're not a bit like a nurse; not a bit like the nurses I had in hospital."

"I had only two years' training in hospital. Since then, I've been looking after people in their own homes. I told you that I didn't rate £70 a week."

"Oh, but you do! You're much better than an ordinary nurse. I can talk to you." She looked at me over the rim of her glass like a solemn child. "It's grim when you can't talk to anyone. You know?"

"Yes. I know."

There hadn't been anyone around to ease my heartbreak after Cecil's final letter. Belle and Mother had both been transparently relieved—in their own interests—that my engagement had been broken.

"Talk away! I'm a good listener," I added encouragingly. "Tell me how you got to know Aylward. Through your father?"

"No. Through Angela . . ."

She told me about the series of studio photographs which her father had wanted taken of her for her eighteenth birthday. Some business associate of her father's had recommended the "De Cointreaux Studio". Angela, I recalled, had reverted to the family's original name for professional purposes. Her studio was becoming quite well known. She'd had her work included in a number of exhibitions. She had also cashed in on Aylward's connections with TV personalities. She didn't care to work in TV studios on a permanent basis, although she had participated in the making of commercials and documentaries for television. She preferred to be independent.

That, I could well believe. I couldn't visualise the imperious, masterful Angela as anyone's employee. Angela possessed the knack of manipulating people. She had been designed to be a puppet master rather than a puppet. She had, from Katy's ingenuous account, pulled Katy's strings subtly and skilfully. Angela had stage-managed the first encounters between Katy and Aylward, and between Aylward and Katy's father. Katy was vaguely aware of Angela's manoeuvres, but Katy saw them as a traditional "fairy godmother's". It was clear that both Katy and her hard-headed father had succumbed to Angela's charm. Angela had contrived to cast her spell over Katy . . . as so many years ago she had cast it over me.

Katy, fresh from boarding-school, with no mother or elder sisters or even any close girl friends to teach her the rudiments of worldly wisdom, must have been as vulnerable as a young dove.

Most girls nowadays were well equipped to take care of themselves, but then most girls were either doing jobs or training for them by the time they were eighteen. Even I, the product of a happy home and a country village, had had a certain knowledge of the realities before I had started my training. Katy seemed to me incredibly naïve and innocent—or ignorant—as if her father's money had esconsed her in a centrally heated glass case. If that case had been shattered on a remote mountainside, it was scarcely surprising that she was still in a state of shock.

For a shrewd business magnate, Harry Haylett must be an utter fool in human relationships. He had virtually invited the attention of wolves to his ewe lamb. He hadn't raised a finger to rescue Katy from Angela's predatory claws. Why not? Had he been impressed by the Decanters' social status? Hadn't he even glimpsed the ruthlessness behind Angela's charm?

Come to that, had I? Hadn't it taken me years to discover that, if she had the sparkle and brilliance of a diamond, Angela had its hardness, too. Perhaps, though I had chafed beneath them during our lunch together, Belle's caustic comments had lingered in my mind. Listening to Katy's disclosures, I was acutely conscious of the part Angela had played in bringing Katy and Aylward together.

"Forcing" would be more appropriate. Angela had spotted, hunted down, and skilfully retrieved Aylward's heiress for him.

That old family joke wasn't funny now, if it ever had been. Granted that, if they were to reclaim and occupy the Hall, the Decanters would need a fortune, couldn't Angela have left the initiative to her twin? Had Aylward seriously desired or intended to "marry money", wouldn't he have done something about it years ago?

Why had he got himself entangled with Katy? She was young and pretty, with a certain heart appeal, but she seemed too young, too immature and inexperienced to captivate a man like Aylward. Perhaps it had been the proposed "Eagle" series which had excited his enthusiasm. Aylward and Angela had been "really thrilled" at the prospect, Katy explained earnestly. The project, even with only a small unit engaged upon it, would be costly, but it would be a prestige programme, which would give Harry Haylett the edge over his business rivals.

It had been cruelly hard luck that the very first of the planned expeditions should have come to grief . . . and "through *me*, though I swear it wasn't my fault", Katy lamented. "Daddy blamed poor Aylward for not having taken better care of me. Daddy was utterly unreasonable. I'll never forgive him for the horrid things he said—or for refusing to wait till Aylward was fit again. Not even Angela could persuade him to postpone the project . . ."

"It's going ahead, is it? Without Aylward?" I said in surprise.

"Oh, yes! Daddy found someone else to head the unit. And Angela went along with him. She said she couldn't break her contracts . . . but I thought it was hatefully disloyal of her. Like—like a rat, leaving a sinking ship. I told her so, and she called me 'a sentimental little nitwit'. She said I could stay behind and hold Aylward's hand, but she had her future to consider."

"I suppose she had a point there."

"I think it was heartless of her. I'll never feel the same way about her again," Katty said miserably. "The grim part is that Aylward doesn't want me to hold his hand. He doesn't recognise me. It's hell . . ."

"Don't I know it?" I interposed hurriedly, as her voice rose. "You offer yourself and your whole future to the man you adore—and he says politely: 'Not today, thank you!' as if he were turning a travelling salesman from his door. D'you suppose any woman on earth—unless she's a born masochist—doesn't go through hell when the door is closed in her face? Grow up, child! You're not unique."

Once again, her eyes widened as she gazed at me.

"You—you are odd," she said uncertainly. "How do you know what it feels like?"

"Ask yourself! Naturally, because I've been through it. The obvious answer is more often than not the correct one," I said wearily. "You're not accepting the obvious where Aylward's concerned, though. You're torturing yourself, searching for way-out answers."

"Am I?" She blinked. "Which is the obvious answer?"

"The doctor's, I would have said. What

was his verdict? Temporary amnesia, following concussion?"

"Yes, but Cecil's a doctor, too, and Cecil says it's psychological. Cecil thinks Aylward wants to forget."

Cecil should have kept his thoughts to himself, I reflected grimly. It had been tactless, if not cruel, to pass them on to Katy.

"To forget the accident, possibly, or the failure of the expedition. Not necessarily to forget *you*," I reasoned. "Anyway, Aylward isn't like that. If he'd made a mistake, he'd own up to it. He wouldn't shrink away from an issue and hide behind loss of memory. Don't you know him at all?"

"Not very well. It all happened so quickly. Really, I've seen much more of Angela than of Aylward," she confessed. "Isn't it odd that you can simply worship a man you hardly know? There's absolutely nothing I wouldn't do for Aylward . . . and I can't even hold his hand."

6

*"Shall I your mirth or Passion move
When I begin to woo?
Will you torment or scorn or love me,
too?"*

THOMAS CAREW

"DO you have to go?" Katy asked fretfully. "You're supposed to be looking after me."

"I have this appointment with Miss Henrietta's solicitor. I have to see him."

"Why?"

"To sign various documents. Miss Henrietta left her car and a few personal possessions to me," I explained.

"What kind of possessions? jewellery? Valuables?"

"I don't think she had anything of any value—just a watch, and a few old-fashioned rings and brooches, plus lots of books, mostly her own novels in various editions."

"Then why bother with her solicitor?" Katy demanded.

"Miss Henrietta was a darling, and she wanted me to have certain keepsakes. It would be ungracious and ungrateful to refuse to take them."

There was a pause. Then, eyeing me critically, Katy went off on a new tack.

"If you're going to see some dry-as-dust old lawyer, why are you all dressed up for him?" she asked suspiciously.

"Because he's neither old nor dusty, and, when I fixed the appointment, he asked me to have lunch with him."

That shook her. She gaped at me.

"He's taking you out to lunch? Why? Have you met him before?"

"On several occasions when he was visiting Miss Henrietta."

"Now, Katy, you mustn't be unreasonable," Mary Decointre interposed. "Constant has promised to come down to Netherfield, but we must give her time to settle her own affairs."

"I don't see why she can't come down with us right away."

"She has told you why not." Mary smiled across the breakfast table at me. "I

94

hope he's a nice young man, Constant. A lawyer should be reliable, but there are exceptions."

I nearly said: "That applies to doctors, too, doesn't it?" but I checked myself.

It was absurd to feel sore because she was looking pleased, as if it was a relief to her to know that I had a man friend. Mothers with eligible, unattached sons were always that way, according to Miss Henrietta. If fathers tended to guard their daughters, mothers could be veritable dragons over their sons, she had assured me. Years ago, Mary Decointre had appeared to welcome my engagement to Cecil . . . but perhaps she had seen it as a safeguard, not a certainty. It had kept Cecil from becoming involved with any other girl during his student years. Perhaps she hadn't expected it to last indefinitely. Perhaps she had planned all along that he should go out to his grandfather in Canada—and marry his talented cousin. She might have expected Cecil to outgrow me, his boyhood sweetheart.

Yesterday evening, Mary had spoken as if I had treated Cecil badly. To a fond mother, the end of our romance might have looked that way. On the other hand, fond mothers rarely admitted that their sons were blameworthy . . . and Cecil had always been his mother's special favourite. She had been ambitious for Cecil. No doubt she still was . . .

Returning her smile, I realised with a pang that I was no longer the "little Conker" of the old days. She would never have suspected Mary Decointre of subtlety or dreamt of querying her motives . . . Even five years ago, that "little Conker" had been as guileless as Katy was now.

"What's he like? He sounds dreadfully dull." Katy was eyeing me reproachfully. "You didn't tell me you had a thing going with a lawyer. Are you planning to marry him?"

"Goodness me, no! He hasn't asked me to marry him," I answered. "We merely happened to meet, through Miss Henrietta, and rather liked each other. When we were talking over the telephone recently, he promised to fix things so that I could have the Cortina transferred to my name right away."

"Second-hand cars aren't worth much,"

Katy said disparagingly. "Didn't the old lady leave you any money?"

"There was no reason why she should have done. I don't suppose she had much, anyway. I thought it was sweet of her to give me her car. Not many people would have thought of it or bothered to make a codicil to that effect," I said warmly. "She put it so nicely, too . . . 'in memory of our pleasant excursions together'. She knew I was saving up for a car of my own."

"Cars are becoming a luxury these days, with insurance and the price of petrol, though in the country they're a necessity," Mary Decointre observed. "Perhaps you could trade in the Cortina for a more suitable car, like a Mini."

That annoyed me. I wasn't quite sure why.

I said: "I happen to like medium to large cars . . . and the Cortina holds some very pleasant memories for me, too. I'd prefer to keep her."

"You won't let that lawyer man keep you, will you? Do you have to lunch with him? I wanted you to help me with my packing," Katy told me. "I hate packing."

"You can't have much to pack. You've been here for only a few days, I gathered."

"Yes, but I've been shopping. The things I've bought won't fit into my suit-cases. What am I to do about them?"

It crossed my mind that, if I was expected to act as Katy's nursemaid and lady's maid, companion and nurse, I should probably earn that generous salary.

It was arranged finally that Mary Decointre should leave for Netherfield Green immediately after lunch, in her Austin 1100. Katy would wait for me, and I would pack her and her belongings into the Cortina.

"You can easily make some excuse not to have lunch with that man," was Katy's parting shot.

I smiled noncommittally. Privately, I had decided that even if Everton didn't implement his tentative invitation, I would have lunch out somewhere. It wouldn't do Katy any good to allow her to behave like ivy and coil herself around me, as if I were a stalwart oak. She was all too obviously the clinging kind, liable to throttle the man she married. For her own sake—and

98

Aylward's—she must be encouraged to stand on her own feet.

I tried to convince myself that I was looking forward to seeing Everton Gillard again. I had certainly enjoyed his visits to Miss Henrietta. It could be that I had exaggerated his interest in me when I had spoken of him to Katy, but I didn't think so. Would he have asked me to lunch with him if he had regarded me solely as a casual, entirely unimportant client? Once I had signed the necessary papers and he had officially handed over the Cortina and those "personal possessions" of Miss Henrietta's, he could surely have dismissed me from his mind? There would be no reason why he should have to remain in touch with me. His invitation must indicate a desire for my company.

I wished, as I walked up the narrow stairs to the solicitors' offices, that my pulses would quicken and my heartbeats become more in evidence. I was twenty-five, unattached, quite personable, and, as far as I knew, perfectly normal. Why, then, couldn't I evince the normal signs common to young women when about to meet an eligible bachelor? I couldn't—

wouldn't—believe that my one frustrated love affair had rendered me immune to any other man's attractions. I had no desire to exude Belle's air of cool indifference, and chill prospective admirers. I wanted to fall in love again.

Only . . . it wouldn't be with this young lawyer. When, with due ceremony, I was shown into his private office and he rose from behind an impressive-looking desk to greet me, my reaction was one of dismay. In his formal dark suit, white shirt and black tie, Everton might have been any rising professional man. I could barely recognise him. If we had met outside in the street, I should probably have walked straight past him.

Granted that he hadn't a memorable face or figure, that he was "medium" or "average" in every way, even to his colouring of light brown hair and grey-blue eyes, I ought, after the hours we'd spent together, to have retained a clearer picture of him. "One who remembers" . . . ? I hadn't remembered Everton in detail. Lack of interest, or lack of emotion, must have blurred the lens of my vaunted photographic memory.

I was ashamed of myself, acutely disappointed, and at a disadvantage. Not even the light clasp of his somewhat fleshy fingers was familiar, as he took my hand in his, and esconsed me in the comfortable padded chair facing the desk.

I was thinking in sudden panic: "He's a stranger. I can't possibly lunch with him. I wouldn't know what to talk about to him. He was quite different at Miss Henrietta's . . . friendly and relaxed and great fun. Why has he gone all formal and professional on me?"

Sensitively, I wondered if this was his method of giving me the "brush-off"; of indicating that he was back in business and no longer in a holiday mood.

Why had I been stupid enough to speak of Everton to Mary and to Katy as if he were a conquest? I glanced at him warily, hoping that I didn't look as humiliated as I felt. He had put on a pair of dark-rimmed glasses and was reading aloud from a formal-looking document. He had a serious, almost severe expression. Even his voice sounded chillier and more precise than in my recollections.

"Point taken. You don't have to

over-emphasise it," I thought resentfully. "What made you imagine that I might try to cash in on our earlier acquaintanceship, anyway? Sheer masculine vanity? Or did you jump to the conclusion that, isolated as I was at Miss Henrietta's, I grasped at you as at a life-line? You were quite wrong, you know. Your visits were merely a pleasant diversion . . ."

He looked up suddenly—and our eyes met.

"You understand?" he inquired.

"Yes. Of course. Fun while it lasted, but no future in it. That was the way I saw it, too," I said defiantly.

His brows contracted until they met over his thin, arched nose.

"I'm afraid I'm not with you," he said. "I'm referring to your legacy from the late Miss Henrietta Pearson . . ."

"The Cortina? Yes. You told me I was to have the Cortina."

"You can't have been listening. Really, Miss Smith, one might imagine that you weren't interested."

"I'm not. In anything personal, I mean. I can't see why you supposed that I was," I said defensively.

"It would appear that we're at cross purposes," he said, with a perplexed stare at me. "Are you trying to convey that you don't wish me—or rather the firm—to act as your legal representative?"

"Heavens, no!" I said in equal bewilderment. "I mean, why should I need a legal representative? I haven't to appear in a law court to answer questions, have I?"

"My dear girl . . ." He made an impatient gesture. "Obviously, you must have a solicitor to look after your interests. I had hoped that you would leave everything to us."

"Yes. Of course. Everything? The probate?" I said vaguely. "That hardly concerns me."

"Naturally, it concerns you. There'll be your proportion of the death duties to be agreed."

"Oh? Shall I have to pay death duties on the Cortina? I hadn't thought of that," I said in dismay.

"Not only on the car. That'll be the least important item. The tricky part will be to arrive at a fair valuation of Miss Pearson's novels."

"You did tell me over the telephone that

she had left me her books. I'd forgotten that," I said in compunction. "It was very kind of her, but she had a great number of books . . . and I haven't anywhere to keep them. Do I have to take them all?"

"Obviously, you misheard—or misunderstood me. I wasn't referring to the actual volumes in the house. Miss Pearson left you all the rights in her novels." He glanced down at the topmost document on his desk. "'In gratitude for her genuine and unstinted help and interest in my work during the time she has spent with me . . .' was how Miss Pearson phrased it. Very nice, too, if I may be permitted to say so, Constant. Or would that be offending your sense of what's fitting?"

"I don't know what you mean," I protested, aware of an aggrieved note in his tone.

"I was under the impression that you were warning me not to—er—introduce a personal note. Putting me in my place, in short."

"Oh, no! I wasn't. I thought *you* were. You seemed so stiff and professional . . ."

"Well, so would *you*, if I were a patient

in your ward. When one's doing one's job, one tries to be business-like."

"Does one? Yes, I suppose one does. . ."

Suddenly, the tension was broken and we were both laughing, a little sheepishly.

"I'm sorry," I said impulsively—apologising for my thoughts rather than for anything I had voiced. "I wasn't concentrating. Do you mean that Miss Henrietta has left her royalties to me?"

"Certainly. All rights in her novels. So . . . you will need a solicitor to look after your interests. I trust, Miss Constant Smith, that I may have the honour and privilege of representing you?"

Now he was being mock formal, and there was a familiar twinkle in his eyes.

"Indeed, yes, Mr. Gillard! I shall be happy to retain your professional services," I answered, in the same tone.

I was still feeling confused as well as relieved. It wasn't until I found myself facing Everton across a table in a discreetly quiet and expensive restaurant that the penny dropped.

"You're talking as if I were an heiress," I said incredulously.

"Why do you sound surprised? You are an heiress," he retorted.

"Oh, to a minor extent, yes! I've inherited Miss Henrietta's dachshund, Cortina, and novels. Scarcely a fortune. The car and Berry—the dog—will cost quite a bit to maintain, and Berry is likely to lose me a number of jobs in the future," I said practically. "I don't suppose my current employer will object to him, but some people might."

"Jobs? My dear, sweet girl, you won't have to worry about jobs. You'll be drawing a comfortable income."

"Are you sure? Miss Henrietta lived so simply . . ."

"From choice, not from necessity." He smiled at me quizzically, his head on one side. "Not what one might call finance conscious, are you, Constant? No curiosity about Miss Henrietta's assets—and dispositions of them?"

"Hardly my business. I wasn't related to her."

"She had no near relatives. After she had made provision for and left generous sums to various old friends, the residue of her money, which is to be divided among a number of animal welfare societies, will amount to around £50,000—less death duties. Surprised?"

"Certainly. Astonished," I said candidly. "I thought she was hard up. I even tried to make the typewriter ribbons and carbons last as long as possible, and I used to wash the car and her undies for her . . ."

"Which she evidently appreciated. She had a tough struggle in her younger days, so she was never inclined to waste money," he said dryly. "Among those letters of hers, which you sent on to the office unopened, were several from her literary agents, containing some advantageous offers for various foreign rights, including one for three titles from Israel."

"Oh? That would have pleased her. I don't think she'd had a book published in Israel before. I can remember how thrilled she was by an offer from a Greek firm . . ." I noted the quirk of his pale eyebrows and went on emphatically: "To a writer, it isn't solely a question of the price. You have to realise that. To acquire a brand-new market is always a thrill, whether there's much money in it or not.

It's the way a dedicated bird-watcher feels when he discovers some hitherto unfamiliar species nesting in his particular preserves for the first time."

"He?" Everton echoed. "*Who*? Have you a dedicated bird-watcher among your admirers?"

"Not among my admirers. I used to know a man who was keen on birds."

"Used to? When?"

"Oh, ages ago! When I was a schoolgirl. I haven't seen him for five years," I said hurriedly.

"Yet you remember him . . . vividly enough to change colour when questioned about him. How come?"

"'How come?' to you," I retorted tartly. "Of what interest can my highly retentive memory be to you?"

"That's an awkward question. If I answer truthfully that everything which concerns you is of interest to me, I'm sticking my neck out for your little axe," he said wryly. "You could tell me not to become personal—or you could suspect me of undue interest in your legacy."

"I could, perhaps, but I wouldn't."

"Sure? That's encouraging. Is it intended to be?"

"I don't know. I mean, I can't see what difference my legacy can make to anyone. It isn't as though I've inherited a portfolio of stocks and shares. Miss Henrietta has gone—and interest in her books may fade."

"Not in your lifetime—at a guess. I gathered that her publishers were about to reprint all her earlier titles in a uniform edition. If that comes off, there'll certainly be plenty of new offers for those half-forgotten titles, and you'll do very nicely out of them."

"So—?"

"Why pretend that money makes no difference? It always makes a difference," he said frankly. "Some of your so-called 'romantic' heroes may shy away from girls with money. Most hard-working professional men are relieved if their wives aren't dependent on them for every cent. Inevitably, it's an additional attraction."

"Yes? I suppose it may be . . ."

"Not that you yourself need money to enhance your very considerable powers of attraction—but it is an embellishment. It'll bring your doctor friend to the point, unless I'm much mistaken. Hell!" he said. "Have I hit the target? You're blushing . . . Then, you are keen on that raw-boned Scot?"

"*What?* What raw-boned Scot?" I asked blankly.

"You're forgetting that I met him . . . at Miss Henrietta's. I saw instantly that he had a proprietary interest in you."

"Oh, Alistair? You're talking about Alistair McCanning?"

"Certainly." His eyes narrowed. "Don't tell me that you've two Scots doctors at your feet."

"There's nobody at my feet, as far as I know. It's the last place I would want to find a man, anyway. Most inconvenient," I said with forced lightness.

"Then, where will you have me?" he asked significantly, "This isn't a game, Constant. I'm in deadly earnest."

7

*"If I should meet thee
After long years,
How should I greet thee?"*

LORD BYRON

"WHAT'S in that big envelope?" Katy inquired, with undisguised curiosity.

"Letters—from Miss Henrietta's publishers and literary agents. Everton wants me to answer them. I had been acting as her secretary, so I'm familiar with her records," I explained.

"I don't see why you should have to bother. You're looking after me now," she protested, with an unmistakable touch of jealousy. "Father won't be paying you to clear up that old lady's affairs."

I pressed my lips tightly together. I had nearly yielded to the impulse to tell her that her father could keep that handsome salary as far as I was concerned. It would have been a gratifying moment . . . but I

111

knew I should regret it, afterwards. Katy wasn't simply a spoilt child who rated a sharp slap. She had been badly shocked and shaken, and was suffering now from a haunting sense of insecurity. She needed skilled understanding, help and encouragement if she wasn't to become a confirmed neurotic. For Aylward's sake—and his mother's—I had to do what I could for Katy.

So I said mildly: "I don't normally start a new job in the middle of the week. I'm stretching a point by driving you down to Netherfield Green. I must have a day or two more in Cornwall—perhaps at the weekend—to clear up things there and collect Berry."

"Berry? Who's Berry?"

"Miss Henrietta's dachshund. She left the cats to her housekeeper, who dotes on them, but she wanted me to have Berry. He's quite young, and a lively little fellow."

"A dog?" she said, as she might have said "a white elephant". "What can you do with a dog?"

"Keep him with me. If a prospective

employer objects, then I'll find one who doesn't," I said firmly.

She puckered her brows over that, eyeing me sideways as if to gauge whether I were in earnest or not.

"You'd pass up a well-paid job—for a dog?"

"Of course. Miss Henrietta trusted me to take care of Berry."

"Oh, well, I don't mind!" she conceded. "I've never had a dog, but Aylward likes dogs, so I'll have to get used to them sometime."

"I suppose you've never had a kitten, either, or anything that's dependent on you?"

She shook her fair head.

"You can come down to Cornwall with me, if you like. It'll be a change for you," I suggested. "Right now, let's finish your packing and head for Netherfield Green."

In my first glimpse of it, I was surprised how little the village had changed. The village green and the chestnut trees, the church, the vicarage, and the inn were exactly as I had remembered them. It was when I drew level with my old home that I became conscious of the differences. The

Forge was a working forge no longer. It had been transformed into an "olde worlde" teashop. That gave me a horrid pang. Presumably, Netherfield Green had run out of blacksmiths. My father hadn't had a son to carry on his family traditions.

The Squire had had two sons, but neither of them had been in a position to carry on at the Hall, I reminded myself. The historic old mansion might look much the same outwardly, but its setting had undergone drastic alterations. The straggling woods around it had been cleared and replaced by new, orderly plantations of conifers. The old-fashioned, overgrown shrubberies and herbaceous borders had been cut back severely and turned into neat, formal beds.

Nowhere now for children to play "hide and seek" or "cowboys and Indians", I thought, an absurd lump in my throat. I wished I hadn't yielded to the impulse to turn in at the side gate and drive past the Hall itself to the main gates and the Lodge, now occupied by Mary Decointre.

"What's the matter?" Katy asked suddenly. "You look as if you could cry."

"I could cry . . . at the way vandals

have treated these gardens. Who's responsible for all this cutting down?"

"The tenants. United Fertilisers Confederation, or UFC, as my father calls it. A very big and important company. They have sets of offices in the house, and they have the gardens as an advertisement for their fertilisers," Katy enlightened me. "The gardens are lovely in the summer months. Haven't you seen them on colour TV? In the commercials?"

"I've never watched colour TV . . ."

"Haven't you? How odd! We have one for ourselves and one for the staff, and I've a portable set of my own," she told me. "UFC are good tenants. They'd buy the Hall if it wasn't entailed. I wanted Daddy to get rid of them, so that Aylward and I could live at the Hall, but Daddy said that would mean that he'd have to give Mrs. Decointre an allowance. She relies on the rent from the Hall."

"I shouldn't think Aylward would care to live there now. The woods, and the shrubberies where we used to find birds' nests, have gone. So have the hawthorn hedges and the ivy on the walls. There can't be a lot of birdlife left around the house."

"Who wants birds to build nests on house walls? Birds are such messy creatures," Katy said, wrinkling up her nose. "Some are quite pretty, but I prefer them at a distance."

"Aylward doesn't. He used to spend hours watching them. He had a tame robin which fed from his hand . . . and a chaffinch which would perch on his shoulder . . ."

I checked myself abruptly, but I couldn't obliterate the vivid memories which had thrown themselves on to my mental screen as we'd passed the Hall. I hadn't consciously thought of Aylward and his tame birds for years. Now I could see that young Aylward poised on one knee outside the potting shed, hand outstretched without a tremor, watching with an eager, absorbed expression, as the robin had perched on his wrist and fed from the palm of his hand. Angela had photographed him like that—and had won a competition in a magazine, in the "under sixteen" section, for the result.

He hadn't shown Angela the robin's

nest, though, in a rusted tin on the shelf of the potting shed. He had shown it to me —and vowed me to secrecy. Angela would want to photograph the nest, and she might frighten the birds away from it, he had explained gravely.

"Aylward and his birds . . ." had been a wry joke among the Decanters. The Squire's sole interest in birds had lain in the preserving—and shooting—of game birds. Mary Decointre had complained, half humorously, half seriously, that Aylward was perpetually raiding the larder for tit-bits for his pets—and that, in return, they devoured her crocuses and polyanthus. Cecil held that birds were destructive to farm and orchard crops, and were liable to carry diseases. Angela had tolerated the photogenic species, but had found bird-watching too much a test of patience for her restless vitality.

So, when Aylward had made an exciting discovery, and had been burning to share it with someone, he had confided in my father and me. My father had had a deep love for the countryside, and for its furred and feathered denizens. He had encouraged me to be observant . . . and sometimes I'd had the satisfaction of revealing one of my discoveries to Aylward. Cecil had been my constant companion and, later, my sweetheart, but Aylward had been my hero from the first.

The Lodge might have been renamed the Dower House. It had been intensively enlarged, many generations ago, for the widowed mother of the reigning Squire. It had continued in use as the Dower House until the "old" Squire's time. Then, lacking any relatives to occupy it, he had allowed it to remain empty. Mary Decointre had hoped to let it as a "holiday cottage". She and the Squire had had it overhauled, and furnished with surplus furniture from the Hall. There had been occasional tenants, but the project hadn't prospered. Perhaps Netherfield Green wasn't near enough to the coast to attract holidaymakers.

There was nothing makeshift in the furnishings in the Lodge now. They had obviously been chosen with care. I recognised many old favourites from the Hall. Rather too many, in fact. The moderate-sized rooms seemed over-full of furniture.

Mary Decointre had tea all ready for us. She greeted me warmly, as if relieved that I hadn't changed my mind. She had looked in at St. Cyriac's on her way home and been told that Aylward should be able to leave hospital next Wednesday.

"Did he say anything? Did he ask for me?" Katy demanded eagerly. "Is he glad about coming home?"

"He scarcely spoke." That pucker of anxiety, which was already becoming familiar to me, contracted Mary's brows. "It is unlike Aylward to be so subdued. It's as though that concussion had crushed his ability to think and feel. Have you ever known a similar case, Constant?"

"I know that a really severe shock can affect people that way. Some people become madly vociferous or hysterical. Others go all silent, as if paralysed," I said slowly, trying to recall the experiences of my training years.

Those years seemed half a lifetime away now. My memories of work on the wards were fading, like ancient photographs. Even the snatched, hurried interludes with Cecil were less vivid than they had been. In contrast, my memories of childhood days were as clear as ever. Particularly, of course, those early memories of the Decanters on their sleek, spirited, wellbred ponies, the familiar jingle of harness, the clip-clop of hoofs, and the at first unfamiliar Western accents . . .

Sweet, bitter-sweet, exciting, frustrating or wholly delightful, those memories should by now have been laid away with lavender bags, I told myself wryly on the following afternoon when, at Katy's insistence, I drove her over to the hospital. Instead, I had gone on wearing them like the rosary in that old Victorian ballad. "Each hour I spent with thee, dear love . . ." I quoted in silent mockery. "Each hour a pearl . . ."

Surely, few girls of my age and generation were so sickeningly sentimental? Did any of us ever bother to pick lavender and make lavender bags? I didn't even care for the scent of it. Always, it reminded me of cats. Well, perhaps that was why I wore my memories strung together, instead of tidied away in a drawer. It could be that I wore the "pearls" as a talisman, to ward off the danger of being hurt all over again.

120

I had successfully avoided any second emotional involvement.

Yes, but if I was afraid of being hurt, why had I answered Mary Decointre's advertisement? Just how inconsistent could I be? I wondered, as Katy grabbed my arm with an impatient: "Not that way . . ."

"Sorry! Force of habit," I explained. "I've never been into the hospital by the visitors' entrance."

"But . . . it must be simply ages since you were a nurse here," she protested. "Habit?"

"Old habits die hard. With me, at any rate." As we neared the open glass doors of the main entrance, I hung back. "Are you sure you want me to come in with you? I could wait in the car. Wouldn't you rather be alone with Aylward?"

"Oh, no! I couldn't bear it. Not while he doesn't know me. It's too grim," she blurted out wretchedly. "He just lies there —not speaking. If I try to talk to him, he answers in a ghastly, polite, puzzled way. It's as if his mind's a blank."

"That must be grim . . ."

I couldn't picture Aylward devoid of his

lively, flashing intelligence, and easy good humour. I suppose, in spite of all Katy and Mary Decointre had told me, I was still expecting to see the dashing young hero of my treasured memories.

The confrontation would have been less of a shock had he been in bed. One expected patients to look pale and ill when they were in bed. Instead, clad in shirt and slacks beneath a dark green and red plaid dressing-gown, he was lying in a long wicker chair, in a corner of the big sun lounge, where the more mobile men patients were wont to gather of an afternoon. Four men quite near him were seated around a small table, playing cards. Three others were watching a race meeting on a portable TV set. Another, younger group, had a radio on, broadcasting pop music at full blast.

All this I took in at a glance—and at a glance I was acutely conscious of Aylward's isolation. He was lying on one side, his back to the other patients, one hand to his forehead, as if to shield his eyes from the sun which was shining through the big picture windows. He wasn't lying in a relaxed attitude, like a cat's in the sunshine. I could sense the tautness in every line of his long, lean frame. He didn't stir as we approached him; didn't open his half-closed eyes.

His pallor, the thinness of that familiar, once beloved face, and the purple shadows beneath the long, sweeping black eye-lashes, clutched at my heart-strings. I had a crazy impulse to fling myself down on my knees beside his chair, to cradle his head against my shoulder, to stroke his over-long dark hair, and murmur reassuring endearments. I had never expected to feel this surge of compassion and fierce protectiveness towards Aylward, my hero, my dashing knight on horseback. It caught me off my guard, like the back-wash from a giant wave.

My heart was thudding, my throat was suddenly dry, and my knees were quivering. Had I been alone, perhaps I should have been carried away by that impulse— as if only physical contact could speak for me and my rush of emotion. I had no words with which to greet him. I stood there, silent and stricken. I had never before felt more miserably inadequate.

Katy dropped my arm and moved

forward in a little rush, pulling up two garden chairs with a clatter and sinking awkwardly into one of them.

"Hello, darling! How are you? Feeling better? Well, you must be, if you're coming home next week," she burst out, in a high-pitched, nervous tone. "You'll be glad to get home, won't you? Or . . . does it fret you to be so near the Hall and yet not living there? You've never said . . ."

Slowly, and as if he were infinitely weary, he turned his head. Then, still as if it required a tremendous effort, he struggled to raise himself into a sitting position. Katy watched him uneasily. I couldn't just stand and watch. I could feel the pain in him as if it were my own. I supposed nursing had the effect of heightening one's perceptions. Hadn't I always known when Miss Henrietta was in pain or acute physical discomfort, bravely though she had sought to hide it?

I said: "Steady there! Let me give you a hand . . ." and bent over him swiftly.

Once he had seemed to me as tough as cow-hide and as solid as granite. Now, I was conscious of his boniness and loss of weight. Indignation swept over me as I helped him into an upright position and piled the cushions up at his back.

"Oh, my dear heart, what have they been doing to you? You're nothing but skin and bones," I cried out involuntarily.

"My dear heart" had been one of my mother's favourite phrases. Why it should have sprung to my lips now, I couldn't imagine . . .

The long lashes flickered. As I stepped back, to the chair Katy had drawn up for me, Aylward looked directly at me. For a moment, it was a baffled, challenging look. Then, his furrowed brow smoothed itself out and the old warm and warming light flashed into his eyes.

"Heavens above, it's Conker! It's the little Conker, home again," he ejaculated. "At long last! Wherever have you been all this time, sweetheart?"

It hadn't occurred to me to wonder whether or not he would recognise me. I had taken it for granted that he would. That he should greet me as "Conker" was no shock. What did shake me was the unfeigned delight in his tone and glance.

"Hello! It's good to see you again," I

said, and thought that must qualify as an entrant for the mis-statement of the year.

It wasn't "good" at all, to see him like this—metaphorically beaten down to his knees. It was heart-rending and infuriating and devastating.

"Where have you been?" he persisted. "Why did you vanish like that? What had we done?"

"I didn't vanish. I was nursing Mother. In Devon. You knew that," I countered. "After her death, I had to find a job. I went down to Cornwall to look after an old lady."

"Without leaving any address. Cutting yourself off from us completely," he reproached me. "Why?"

"But . . . I didn't. Belle knew where I was. If you'd wanted my address, you could have asked her for it . . ."

"Belle? So . . . it was Belle?" he said, as if to himself. Then, a travesty of his old gay smile lit up his thin face. "No matter. We've found you again. Don't tell me you've come back to St. Cyriac's just as I'm to be discharged?"

"Oh, no! I don't think I could stick hospital life again. I'm looking after our

126

young friend here. Katy," I added emphatically, as he glanced from me to her.

For the life of me, I couldn't add: "Your fiancée." Because, if she was his betrothed, she oughtn't to be, I thought confusedly. He wasn't in love with her. He didn't feel anything towards her. I knew that. I could feel it right through me. Whatever had or hadn't happened to Aylward, Katy was extraneous to it.

"Katy?" he echoed, and his dark eyes were charged with a sudden, urgent appeal. "Yes. She's been here before. To visit me. I can't quite make out why . . ."

"Oh, Aylward! Oh, darling, don't! Can't you see that you're breaking my heart?" Katy's voice was shaking as if with passionate emotion and tears were welling up in her eyes. "Why can't you remember? Oh, you must remember me! It's cruel of you to pretend that you don't."

"I'm not pretending," he said defensively. "I know you've been here before with my mother."

"You've remembered her—" with a resentful, suspicious glance at me. "And,

127

according to her, you haven't seen her for five whole years."

"Five years? It seems even longer. Doesn't it, Conker? A whole lifetime since that ghastly accident . . ."

"You've remembered the accident?" Katy intervened quickly.

"To Constant Smith . . . Conker's father. I've never forgotten it . . . never stopped kicking myself because I wasn't there. I'd meant to ride down with Angela, but a girth had snapped . . . and she wouldn't wait for me."

"I didn't mean that. I meant my accident . . . our accident," Katy said, in a hurt tone. "How can you have forgotten that grim night? I can't forget it. I keep on having nightmares. They're making me quite ill. That's why Nurse Smith is here . . . to look after me. We hired her yesterday."

The furrows smoothed out again—and again he smiled at me.

"Conker's looking after you? That's grand news! She'll soon put you right, and clear up all this mystery," he said.

"Mystery?" Katy echoed doubtfully.

"Well, it is, isn't it? I expect the

solution lies with my brother. Whenever there's a mystery, he's usually at the bottom of it. He's clever, and he has that tortuous kind of mind that's difficult to follow—or to anticipate," he said, his dark head moving restively against the cushions. "Too deep for me . . . and for Conker, too, I guess. Like La Belle Blonde. She was perpetually driving wedges—in secret. Promising to forward letters . . . and then conveniently forgetting . . ."

His voice, with its all too familiar accent, seemed to trail off as if from exhaustion. It came home to me, in dismay, that he was still a sick man.

I said reluctantly: "I think we've talked enough—" just as Katy burst out with: "What on earth do you mean? You're not talking sense. What has Cecil to do with it? And who's 'La Belle Blonde'? You can't mean me . . ."

He shook his head in a helpless, desperate gesture.

"Oh, lay off him, Katy!" I said bluntly. "Can't you see that he's exhausted? Wait till he's at home again. Then, we shall have all the time in the world to straighten things out between you."

"Between us," he agreed—but he was looking directly at me . . . not at Katy. "All the time in the world? How good that sounds! Life has been such a frantic rush . . . and for what? Like a confounded treadmill. I've had it, Conker."

"I know, I *know*, but it's over now. Just relax. Nobody's going to force you into anything . . . except over my dead body," I promised him.

"That sounds like my Conker. You won't run away again? Running away leaves everything unfinished . . ." he said ruefully. "This time, you must stay and see things through . . ."

"Yes," I said. "Yes, I will. Not to worry, dear heart. As Mother used to say, it'll all come out in the wash."

8

*"The days may come, the days may
  go,
But still the hands of memory
  weave,
The blissful dreams of long ago."*
GEORGE COOPER

ONLY . . . I hadn't run away;
hadn't tried to vanish. What had
Cecil said, to give his brother that
erroneous impression? What had Belle
said? What had Belle done?

I had never, even in my blackest
moments, when I had been devastated by
heartbreak over Cecil, wanted to cut
myself off from the whole family. The
"cutting off" process had been their
choice, their doing, not mine—or so I had
imagined until now. Now, with Aylward's
searching, reproachful glance on me, I had
to absolve him at least of any wish to
banish me from his family circle. Love
might have failed me, but friendship

131

hadn't. Aylward was still staunchly my friend.

I was warmly grateful to him; so much so that I was in no mood to measure my words or gestures. Katy had bent over him and kissed him a reluctant "goodbye for now". Unthinkingly, I followed her example.

I had intended to plant a light, sisterly kiss on his forehead. Instead, I found my hands caught in a firm grasp, and found myself pulled towards him so that our lips met.

His lips seemed to reach out for mine and cling to them, as if to the proverbial life-line. I could feel his desperate need of security and reassurance. How could I not respond to it?

Aylward had always been dear to me— a very special person—even when I'd had my parents to care about me and Cecil constantly at my side. Now, my parents had gone, Cecil had walked out on me, and, apart from that slender blood-tie between us, Belle was virtually a stranger. To have Aylward back again, no longer a gilded image in a niche to be worshipped in secret, but a live man, who had been sorely battered and needed a helping hand, was a bliss of which I had never even dreamt. I was in no state to gauge that warm, rapturous lift of my heart or to foresee danger in it.

Whatever Aylward wanted of me, he could have. It was as simple as that. Hadn't I taken enough from him in the past? He had always been a generous and spontaneous giver, never looking for any return. How could I measure out my response to him now?

What I murmured to him was hopelessly trite . . . the smallest of small coins . . .

"Just relax . . . you must get fit again . . . That's all that matters. No, of course I won't vanish—if I ever did. I'll be there, waiting for you . . . I'll be helping your mother to take care of you . . . We'll soon have you fighting fit."

What he said, very low, as he released me, was of more precious metal . . .

"My little Conker . . . bless you, sweetheart! There was never anyone else to touch you. There never could be . . . You've come back at last, and I'll never let you go again . . ."

133

His soft drawl echoed and re-echoed in my ears as I walked beside Katy back to the car park. Bemusedly, I was struggling to sort out the tangled emotions which were whirling around crazily, as if my brain were a spin dryer. I would have had to admit—shameful confession from a nurse—that I wasn't sparing a thought for Katy. I did notice that she was looking flushed and disturbed, but I imagined that I was, too. One would have had to have been made of steel and concrete not to have reacted to that change in Aylward.

She managed to contain herself until we had settled ourselves in the Cortina. Then, before I could switch on the ignition, the storm broke. I was totally unprepared. I just gaped at her.

When, finally, she ran out of breath or invective or both, I said confusedly: "But . . . I haven't lied to you. I told you the truth. I was never in love with Aylward. I wouldn't have dared to feel that way about him. He was the future Squire . . . the Prince Charming of the family . . . someone quite super and out of my orbit, when Mother and I left Netherfield Green. Besides, I was engaged to Cecil."

"I don't believe you! How can I believe you, when I saw the way he looked at you and heard the way he spoke to you?" Katy blazed. "You're a fraud . . . a cheat. You wormed yourself into this job just to be near Aylward."

"Oh, heavens! Ask Mary Decointre about my love life. Ask Angela. They'll tell you that I was going to marry Cecil . . . until he went out to Canada and changed his mind about me," I retorted in exasperation.

"Why? Why did he change his mind? Because he found out that you were carrying on with his brother?"

"No. I imagine that he was tired of waiting. I was tied down, looking after an invalid mother. I never even saw Aylward after we'd moved to Devon. 'Carrying on', indeed? Where did you pick up that cheap phrase?"

She flinched and glowered at me through a mist of tears.

"Are you finding fault with the way I talk? I thought you were the village blacksmith's daughter . . . and went to the village school."

"My education didn't begin and end

there. For the last three years I've been working for a novelist who knew how to use words, and hated them to be cheapened." With an effort, I checked my rising temper. "Listen, Katy! I'm sorry if I did or said anything to give you the wrong impression. I was so shocked and distressed to see Aylward in that condition that I didn't think about anyone or anything else."

"I don't know what you mean. In that condition?" she echoed blankly. "But . . . he's much better. He's almost himself again, apart from the loss of memory."

"Don't! If that's true, it makes it worse. Because he simply isn't Aylward . . . the Aylward I knew. All the gaiety and sparkle, the warm enthusiasm, and that endearing sense of humour have been knocked out of him—or at least laid flat."

"Well, he isn't back to normal yet, or he would remember me." She fumbled for her handkerchief and dabbed at her streaming eyes. "I'm s-sorry. I didn't mean to fly out at you . . . but it shook me up that he should have remembered you . . . and even called you by that absurd pet-name."

"We might have expected it. I gather that it's only the immediate past which he has forgotten," I reminded her. "Cheer up, now! When he's at home again . . ."

"D'you suppose that'll make any difference? He doesn't react to me at all. Didn't you see that?"

I nodded. There was suddenly an uncomfortable lump in my throat. As soon as he was at home again, they would be making demands on him . . . his mother and Angela and Katy. They wouldn't give him the peace he so sorely needed.

I wished fervently that I could carry him off in my car to that isolated cottage of Miss Henrietta's. His wounds—whatever they were—would have a chance to heal there, in that peaceful silence, broken only by the surge of waves, the cries of seagulls, and occasional barks from Berry. Peace? Such an incongruous word in connection with Aylward—and yet I had sensed that his every nerve was crying out for it.

"I don't understand you," Katy said fretfully. "You say you were engaged to Cecil—but you've hardly spoken of him. All your concern seems to be for Aylward."

"True," I said, startled by her perspicacity. "Perhaps one reaches a stage when one can't agonise any more over a lost love. There must be a limit of some kind to any suffering. Beyond that limit, one would simply curl up and die."

"You felt that way over Cecil?" she said incredulously. "He's nice, of course, and clever, too, but he isn't exciting. He doesn't send me. Don't you care about him any longer?"

"I don't know," I answered truthfully.

"You certainly care about Aylward."

"Oh, don't start that again! Aylward was my friend, not my sweetheart, and he never hurt me. He was always kind." I saw the sceptical glance she shot at me, and added: "Kindness is terribly important. You'll find that out when you're older. It's something everyone needs, but no one can buy. It's like 'mercy' in Portia's speech . . . 'the gentle dew from Heaven'. Perhaps they're much the same thing."

"You talk in the most peculiar way. Not like a nurse . . ."

"I warned you that I was an amateurish

sort of nurse. I never learned the professional jargon."

"You're not like a village blacksmith's daughter, either."

"Oh, Katy, you sound so young! You can't label and file people away in neat dockets. Why should I be like this or like that? I'm myself."

"Some people are—like what they're meant to be," she said obstinately. "Cecil's like a doctor, and Aylward was like a TV personality is supposed to be."

"Even on TV, Aylward always seemed himself to me; perfectly natural," I demurred. "I dare say it was a strain on him, though. He never cared for the limelight."

"It would have been madness not to have cashed in on his popularity. D'you know, he was offered the job of Warden at one of those new nature reserves? It was miles from anywhere, with just a cottage and pretty poor pay. He thought it sounded inviting, but we all told him it wouldn't do."

"Oh? You all told him?"

Anger was rising in me again like a fierce flame. I pressed my lips tightly together. Aylward wasn't my concern. If he chose to let himself be "told" what to do by his womenfolk, that was his own lookout. He could have stood up to them.

Why was I convinced that a Warden's job would have suited him down to the ground? He might be sold on that "TV personality" game. He might have been bored to distraction at Miss Henrietta's. Why should I have such a clear vision of him in that lonely cove below the cottage, sprawled out on the warm sand, binoculars to his eyes, smiling as he watched the seabirds on the cliffs above?

I couldn't picture Katy in that setting— or Cecil, either. Perhaps one knew intuitively more about dear friends than about adored sweethearts; saw them "au naturel" and stripped of all pretences. One didn't "put on an act" for a trusted friend. One let down one's hair, confident of being understood and forgiven. Before a lover, one was apt to preen and show off one's best paces.

I couldn't see Katy at Miss Henrietta's, but she appeared determined not to let me out of her sight. She insisted on accepting that casual invitation to accompany me.

"It means a long drive. Are you sure you feel up to it?" Mary Decointre asked her. "You're still looking frail."

"I shan't look—or feel—any better for staying here, brooding. I'm not going to that hospital again—to be treated as if I were a Health Visitor or a Social Worker or something," Katy retorted stormily. "As Constant said, there are limits to what one can take. Perhaps I shall end by not caring two straws what happens to Aylward—and then goodbye to his hope of getting back the Hall. It would serve him right if he never did live there again."

"Oh, my dear child, you mustn't upset yourself like this! You must remember that the poor boy has been desperately ill," Mary said swiftly. "You might remember, too, how he received those injuries . . ."

Two bright spots of colour showed over Katy's rounded cheekbones. She glowered at Mary.

"Blame me for the whole thing! That's the easy way out. Don't ask yourself why I fell—or who was responsible," she flashed. "You'd do or say anything to cover up for your precious family, but they're not fluffy baby chicks now, to be gathered under your wings, or be fed choice morsels from your beak."

Katy, as I had already noted, had at times a kind of innate, child-like perspicacity. As Mary flinched, I found myself wondering if she—or Angela—had seen Katy as a "choice morsel" to be handed on to Aylward. Perhaps neither of them was willing to admit that he was no "chick" now, and should be left alone to forage for himself.

Recognising the gathering storm symptoms in Katy's rising colour and voice and Mary's tightened lips, I intervened with: "Why not leave the recriminations till Aylward's memory returns? As for the Cornish trip, it will be a change of scene for Katy. I shall be glad of her company —and you can have a rest while we're away, Mrs. Decointre."

"It's a long journey—and people are apt to drive Cortinas too fast," Mary protested.

"You should worry! If I was killed in a road accident, Aylward would get all my money—and nobody could blame any of you," Katy said acidly.

"My dear . . ." Mary began, in a tone

which warned me that her temper was beginning to fray.

"Oh, sorry! I'm an ill-mannered brat. That's what you think, isn't it?" Katy's voice quavered. "Only—you never see *my* point of view. All you care about is what I can do for your precious sons."

Awkwardly, as if half-blinded by unshed tears, she sprang up and blundered towards the door. Mary didn't attempt to intercept her, but, instead, shrugged her shoulders and cast a wryly resigned glance at me.

"I'm afraid that's what she is, at times —an ill-mannered, spoilt brat," she observed, as the door crashed to behind Katy. "No—" shaking her head as I rose to follow my patient, "don't rush after her to hold her hand. Let her cool down and realise that she's behaving abominably."

I paused irresolutely, scanning her thin, intelligent face, once as familiar and dear to me as my own mother's. She had told me that Katy "clung to" her. She had, in that initial interview, spoken of Katy in what I had taken to be genuine affection and concern. Now, I was beginning to wonder . . .

Perhaps Mary, like my mother, was at heart a "man's woman". She had never been close to Angela, who had been the Squire's favourite. Perhaps it was true that only her sons mattered to Mary. There had been a disconcertingly hard note in her voice when she had spoken to and of Katy. She needn't have reminded Katy of how Aylward had incurred his injuries. Admittedly, Katy hadn't used the kind of words or tone in which a prospective bride would normally address her future mother-in-law, but Katy had been under considerable stress. An understanding woman would have made allowances, not looked as though she would gladly give Katy a good slippering.

"She has been badly hurt," I said tentatively.

"Badly brought up, you mean! She is a brat, when she feels like it," Mary retorted shortly. "I wish to heaven Aylward had landed a girl with some self-control and poise and common sense. I suppose there's not much in him to appeal to a girl of intelligence and sophistication. One outgrows the stage of falling for a good-looking hunk of brawn."

"Is that how you see your elder son?"

I recognised in dismay the biting irony in my tone, but Mary didn't appear to notice it. She had risen and crossed to the sideboard. We had finished tea only about ten minutes ago, but it seemed that Mary felt the need of a more powerful stimulant.

"Mr. Brawn," she said, over her shoulder, with brittle amusement. "Eye-catching in his way—but he'll have less appeal if that tiresome accident leaves him permanently lame. He'd better hang on to Katy. Most heiresses nowadays want to marry men who are good at business, not simply romantic heroes."

"Why does he need an heiress?"

"Surely, the answer's obvious? He'll never get our home back for us off his own bat. It isn't as if he had Cecil's brains or character." Holding up a tumbler half full of whisky, she sank into the nearest armchair. She sipped the drink thirstily. "By the way, Cecil will be here tomorrow evening. You'll be careful, won't you, Conker?"

"Careful? In what way?" I inquired.

"I wouldn't want the boy to be upset again, over you. I haven't told him that you're here. I thought it would be better for you to meet casually, as it were—not to make a thing out of it by warning him."

"The boy?" I thought, with an involuntary curl of my lips. Presumably, to an adoring mother, her sons were always "boys" . . . unless they managed to convince her that they were grown men. Perhaps, normally, it was left to their wives to tackle that onerous task; to frustrate the "mother hen" complex. Katy had the perception to be aware of that complex, but I doubted if she had the experience to deal with it.

"Cecil has a great future ahead of him. Nothing must be allowed to spoil it," Mary added pointedly.

I didn't answer. Suddenly out of harmony with her, I went out, after Katy.

As I had anticipated, Katy was sprawled on her bed, sobbing.

"Look, that's enough!" I said, flopping down on the end of her bed. "Tears don't do much to ease the grimness. They're really just a form of self-indulgence. They won't impress Mary Decointre. They'll merely exasperate her."

"She exasperates *me*," Katy responded,

with a flash of spirit. "Oh, I know I was appallingly rude to her, but she does madden me when she goes into that mother hen act!"

"I should react to it, too," I conceded. "Mothers-in-law may be a hackneyed joke, but there's generally a lot of truth behind that kind of sour humour. You needn't regard yourself as a solitary martyr. Fathers-in-law can be a trial, too. Your fond papa will put Aylward through it."

"My fond papa has washed his hands of me."

"Don't you believe it! That kind of "high dudgeon" is just as much an act. He'll expect to find you properly penitent and eager to be clasped to his manly breast again, on his return from his trip."

"You don't know him." She giggled weakly. "He's more likely to clasp Angela to him. He's a bit of a lad—or so he fancies. Not the male equivalent of Mrs. Decointre by any means. He doesn't look like any girl's 'fond papa'. Well, he's only forty-three, and looks less."

"Oh? I hadn't realised that."

"People don't. They think 'business magnate' and expect a balding head, horn-rimmed glasses, a bulging waistline, and a dictatorial manner. My father has wavy fair hair, bright blue eyes, a slim figure, and a deceptively friendly approach to everyone," she explained. "It spoils his image to have a grown-up daughter, so he's rarely seen in public with me."

"Poor child! You have had it tough," I said feelingly, and she gaped at me.

"You certainly do say the oddest things. All the girls at school envied me madly—for the way Pop looked, as well as for his money. They nicknamed him 'Glamour Boy'."

"I can imagine it. *Glamour?* Who wants glamour in a father—or in a husband, for that matter? Why on earth didn't you hunt around for a nice, reliable, solid oak?"

"Like Cecil, you mean? But . . . he's quite plain, compared with Aylward. Clever, of course, but he jolly well knows it. He makes me feel a fool." Her tears forgotten, as swiftly as a child's, she eyed me curiously. "Are you going to fall in love with him all over again?"

9

"What a little thing
To remember for years—"
WILLIAM ALLINGHAM

I DESPISED myself for "prinking", as my mother would have called it, but wasn't it natural that I should yearn to look my best when I confronted my erstwhile lover again? His mother hadn't warned him of my presence, so, in his first glimpse of me, I should be able to read his verdict.

It would be painfully humiliating if I saw satisfaction and relief—at his narrow escape—in his eyes. At twenty-five, I couldn't hope to whet any man's appetite with that dewy, daisy-fresh, innocent look which was so appealing in Katy. I had, I hoped, gained something over the years, though; a modicum of poise and self-control. In face and figure, I was thinner than I had been as a student nurse, and my freckles were much less in evidence.

My hair was still glossily bronze-red and my eyes were more green than grey.

I was no beauty, but I did possess—as Everton Gillard had assured me—a certain attraction. Slightly off-beat and unconventional, or "odd" as Katy put it, but quite strong where some people—and most animals—were concerned. Miss Henrietta had responded to it, and so had Berry and old Martha.

In my extreme youth, I had envied Belle's blonde, classic beauty, and Angela's striking, flashing good looks and sparkle. Compared with Belle and Angela, I had, it had seemed to me then, little to offer. Close contact with dear Miss Henrietta had lessened my feeling of inferiority. She had given me a new sense of values. I knew now that kindness, compassion, courage and a sense of humour could be greater and more lasting assets than silky fair hair or big dark eyes.

"He's here—" Katy came bounding into my bedroom without any preliminary tap. "He's changed his car. He has a Saab now. He looks very much the successful, rising young GP. Are you feeling all goofy about seeing him again?"

"Curiously enough, I'm not," I said candidly. "I might have expected to be 'all of a flutter', but my pulse is disappointingly normal."

"You look cool enough . . . and quite elegant. That odd shade of green suits you and, of course, you have exceptionally nice long legs," Katy said approvingly. "Perhaps he'll be sorry he dropped you."

"I thought he would have been married to his Canadian cousin long before this," I said. "I wonder why he isn't?"

"I can tell you that." She grinned impishly. "Angela told me. The cousin said Cecil was too conceited—and wanted to scoop the pool before he'd earned it. She convinced the old man she was right —and he left the Clinic to her. Cecil was very hurt about it."

"He must have been. Conceited?" I repeated. "Oh, no! Merely confident. He was nicknamed 'The Brain' before he was eight years old. He could hardly have pretended that he wasn't clever."

"Perhaps she's cleverer. Or perhaps she's a Women's Lib type," Katy suggested. "Anyway, Cecil ought to appreciate your devotion now."

A week ago, I wouldn't have queried her use of the word "devotion". I had supposed that I was still carrying a torch for Cecil. Wasn't I among those described in the song hit as "one who remembers"? There had never been any other man in my life. Until my visit to Everton's office, I amended, half guiltily. Not that I was likely to take Everton seriously, but it wasn't unpleasing to realise that he was serious about me. I didn't want to end my days as a victim of unrequited love. I wasn't the martyr type. Had I lived a less secluded life, I might easily have been married by now.

Katy was young enough to be proud of her whole-hearted "devotion" to Aylward. I was old enough to feel ashamed and humiliated that I hadn't as yet found anyone to take Cecil's place. Possibly, it had been contact with Katy which had made me feel that way. What was understandable and permissible in a girl of eighteen looked to me now like weakness and self-indulgence in a woman of twenty-five.

Head high and shoulders squared, I followed Katy downstairs. I was determined not to give Cecil the impression that I was yearning to pick up the threads and knit them together again.

He was standing with his back to the empty hearth in the over-crowded sitting-room, a glass of sherry in his hand. I looked at him. I stared. Perhaps I gaped.

Five years can mean so much—or so little. I had matured in the last five years, but I hadn't changed. Cecil, to my first startled glance, was barely recognisable. Naturally, I reminded myself crossly, an oncoming GP wouldn't look like a keen, lean, and scruffy medical student. I should have been prepared for a more civilised, mellower version of the old Cecil.

Yes, but I couldn't have anticipated the smoothness of the present-day product; the immaculately styled, glossy brown hair, the impressive-looking, exaggeratedly large, black-rimmed glasses, the rounding of those formerly high, prominent cheek-bones, and the filling out of that once scraggy figure. I couldn't have guessed that he would ever put on weight or go in for a beautifully tailored, obviously expensive, silver-grey lounge suit and a lavender silk shirt with a matching tie.

I stood motionless in the doorway as if paralysed by shock. I had never before realised the significance of that hackneyed phrase—"I couldn't believe my own eyes".

"He does look rather super, doesn't he?" Katy murmured in my ear, as if aware of my reaction but misinterpreting its cause. "He's a dear, though." Grabbing my arm, she dragged me forward, exclaiming: "Hello, there, Doctor! I've found my nurse and she's smashing. Take a good look at her!"

His brows contracted as if he deplored such naïve tactlessness. He turned with a polite, deprecating gesture.

The light was glinting on his glasses so that I couldn't see his eyes, but the dropping of his jaw was comically expressive.

"*What?*" he ejaculated. "*Constant?* Is it Constant Smith? Well . . . this certainly is a surprise . . ."

"Not too great a shock, I hope?" I was pleased to note that my voice sounded calmer and steadier than his. "How are you, Cecil? Not that I need to ask. You look flourishing."

"Oh, yes! I'm doing pretty well, thank you. What about yourself? How do you happen to be here? You're not at St. Cyriac's now . . ."

So—he had taken the trouble to ascertain that? Why? Out of curiosity? Or from an instinct of self-defence?

Surely, not even Katy could imagine that he was glad to see me again. It was painfully evident—at least to me—that he was reacting like a prodded hedgehog.

"No," I said coolly. "I've been doing private nursing since my mother died. I noticed your mother's advertisement and answered it."

"She told me that she had an unexpectedly large number of answers . . ."

He paused abruptly, as if realising that he could scarcely ask: "What on earth made her choose you?"

"Wasn't it lucky? For us, I mean," Katy interposed blithely. "The moment I saw Constant, we seemed to click. She isn't a bit like a nurse. She's much more human than any of those I had in hospital."

"I can imagine . . ." Again, he checked himself. His lips twisted into a wintry smile. "You were never really keen on nursing, were you, Constant? You let yourself be pushed into it. I'm surprised that you haven't turned your attention to something more in the domestic line. You would make an excellent mother's help."

"Do you think so?" My tone was bland. I might have been speaking to a complete stranger. Inwardly, I was flinching. Had he deliberately tried to sting me? "A mother's help", indeed? Had he forgotten all he had ever known about me? "Stable-girl" would have been more appropriate, or even "kennel-maid". "As a matter of fact, for several years I've been secretary, nurse, and chauffeur to a well-known novelist: I doubt if I would be good with small children."

"I was thinking of the mothers. You were so devoted to your own mother."

Did that still rankle? I wondered, with a sense of shock. Would he never forgive me for my refusal to abandon my mother? But . . . if he had really cared for me, he would have gone on waiting, instead of snatching at his freedom.

156

"She left Constant her car, her dog, and her collection of books," Katy told him. "We're going down to Cornwall tomorrow to fetch the dog."

"To Cornwall? I scarcely think that's advisable, my dear. You're not fit enough yet for any great exertion," Cecil pronounced, turning his attention to Katy again. "You've had a trying time."

"You can say that again!" she agreed. "It's not over yet, by a long shot, but Constant makes it less grim. If she goes down to Cornwall, I'm going with her. That's final! Your mother and I are getting on each other's nerves. In fact, I'm driving her to drink."

"You absurd child! Do you have to exaggerate every trifle?" Cecil's tone was that of a benign uncle, and I wasn't surprised that Katy flushed and snapped: "Oh, cut out the bedside manner! She is drinking too much. Isn't she, Constant?"

"What is 'too much', in that sense?" I countered. "It wouldn't be correct to say that Mrs. Decointre is drinking to excess, but she is in a state of nerves, and I doubt if whisky helps to steady her."

"Is that your professional opinion, Nurse Smith?"

He had obviously tried to use a light, teasing tone—as Aylward might have done —but it sounded hollow and brittle from Cecil. He had never had Aylward's innate liveliness and sense of humour. To Cecil, from an early age, "life is real, life is earnest" had been a truism.

The emphasis he had laid on "professional" jarred on me. If he, like Belle, deplored my refusal to go back to St. Cyriac's, why didn't he say so bluntly? Why these not too subtle digs at me? If I lacked the spirit of dedication which Belle had inherited from Mother, I wasn't alone in that. Not every student nurse in my year had finished her training and become an SRN. There had been "drop-outs" for a variety of reasons.

"Oh, don't fuss! I'm not complaining about your mother," Katy interposed again. "I'm just telling you that I'm not staying here without Constant. What's the use, anyway? We went to see Aylward yesterday, and he still hadn't a clue. About *me*, that is. He recognised *her* fast enough."

158

"What's that? You took Constant to visit Aylward?" Cecil looked and sounded perturbed. "That was most unwise."

"Why? It didn't upset him. In fact, he seemed pleased to see her. He called her 'Conker', and kissed her as if she'd been Angela," Katy said naïvely. "I was quite jealous."

"In Aylward's mental condition, any form of shock could result in a set-back. We don't want him to revert to his childhood," Cecil said reprovingly. "That can happen . . . that reversion or rather retrogression. A kind of escapism."

"Is Aylward subconsciously seeking for escape? Why? And from what?" I asked directly.

"From adult responsibilities and decisions," Cecil answered unhesitatingly. "Father's death hit him hard. He didn't want to have to be the head of the family; to have to part with our home and to be left to sink or swim on his own. You must remember how dependent he was on Angela years ago. Without her to goad him and tell him what to do, poor old Aylward was like a ship adrift."

"He doesn't appear to have done too

badly, all the same," I said, irritated by the note of disparagement in his tone. "He comes across well on television. I always thought he gave in to Angela years ago because he was naturally easy-going, not because he was spineless."

"Much the same thing in this instance."

"I don't know. Lots of husbands humour bossy wives simply because they see no point in fighting over trifles," I protested.

The tension was broken by Mary Decointre, who emerged from the kitchen looking flushed and harassed.

"So sorry to hold you all up like this. I'd managed to get some fresh trout, and I was trying to make a special sauce of which Cecil is particularly fond," she explained hurriedly. "One of those eggs I had from the supermarket was bad—so I had to throw the sauce away and start over again."

"You shouldn't have gone to all that trouble for me," Cecil said, with an indulgent smile. "Remember, I'm not a half-starved student now. We feed pretty well at Dr. Kay's."

"So I would imagine," I said sweetly. "You look quite sleek with good living."

"Dr. Kay and his wife think a great deal of Cecil," his mother proclaimed proudly. "He has his own rooms in their house, but he takes most of his meals with them, and Cecil says she's a cordon bleu cook. I'm afraid I can't compete."

Such meals as I had partaken of at the Lodge, to date, had certainly been undistinguished. A woman from the village came in for a few hours of a weekday morning and prepared the midday meal. Supper consisted of a light snack, cooked by Mary Decointre. Breakfast—toast, coffee and fruit-juice—was produced by the one of us who came downstairs first.

I hadn't foreseen that Mary would want to lay on "dinner" for Cecil, or I would have offered to help. From Mother and from Miss Henrietta's Martha, I had learned enough to call myself a reasonably good "plain" cook.

At the Hall, of course, the Decanters had had an adequate staff to cook and clean for the family. Perhaps Mary had never had to wrestle with a kitchen stove until she had moved to the Lodge. Mother

161

had held that good cooking was mainly a matter of using one's common sense, but Mary evidently cherished illusions of grandeur.

The "game" soup was obviously of the expensive tinned variety, liberally diluted. The trout had been grilled for too long; presumably while Mary had been concocting the sauce. The sauce itself was pleasantly flavoursome but a shade lumpy. The salad which accompanied the fish looked attractive, but the lettuce leaves had lost their crispness and the cooked beetroot was bullet hard. The "sweet" consisted of a large block of a commercially made ice-cream—a rum-and-raisin variety, garnished with bought meringues.

Cecil had two generous helpings of ice-cream. Evidently, he had retained the "sweet tooth" of his early years. I could remember the time when most of his weekly pocket-money had gone on ice-cream cornets from the village stores. Angela had usually been saving up for a new film. Aylward had bought peanuts, which he'd shared with his semi-tame birds, and I had bought packets of loaf sugar for the ponies or potato crisps for myself. That Saturday morning trip to the village stores, with our newly acquired pocket-money, had been one of the events of the week. I hadn't thought of it for years, but it came back to me now as I watched Cecil's diving into his second portion of ice-cream.

Had it been typical of Cecil, even in those days, that he had chosen something he couldn't be expected to share? Aylward had invariably offered Angela and me some of his peanuts, and I had reciprocated with my potato crisps or packets of sugar.

The conversation over dinner could scarcely have been called inspired or inspiring. It had been mainly on impersonal topics; held there firmly by Cecil and his mother, I had perceived. A discussion of the soaring costs of running a car had led, as we were waiting for Cecil to finish his ice-cream, to Mary Decointre's reiterated opinion that I would be well advised to trade in Miss Henrietta's Cortina for a smaller car.

"It's absurd to wax sentimental over a car," Mary declared. "I'm sure your lawyer friend will agree. You don't have to keep that Cortina simply because the old lady left it to you."

"What lawyer friend?" Cecil asked quickly.

"Oh, he's Connie's newest admirer!"

From Mary's tone and smile, anyone might have imagined that I collected "admirers" as some people collect postage stamps. She proceeded to regale Cecil with those scraps of information about Everton which she had managed to elicit from me. They didn't strike me as impressive, but Cecil received them with an expression of acute distaste.

I had an impulse to warn Mary: "Be careful! Don't you know your own son? Can't you see that you're not putting him off me? You're arousing the competitive urge . . ."

I had, indeed, barely swallowed my coffee before that urge manifested itself.

"It's a pleasant night. Let's take a stroll, Conker," Cecil said—and it was more of a command than an invitation.

Perhaps there was a slight quickening of my pulses in response, but I asked bluntly: "*Why?*"

"*Why?*" He looked momentarily taken

aback. Then, swiftly, he took refuge behind his professional manner: "If you're determined to carry Katy off to Cornwall, there are certain precautions you should take . . ."

10

"He found it inconvenient to be poor."

WILLIAM COUPER

CECIL was more subtle than his mother. By hinting that he wanted to talk to me about Katy's welfare, he had blocked any attempt on his mother's part to send Katy with us.

"We shan't be long," Cecil pronounced, with a propitiating smile at Mary. "There are just a few things we need to get straight. Constant appears to have dived into this job without any preliminary briefing."

The implication was that I had been desperate for a job and had snatched at this one; possibly, even that I had begged for it "for old times' sake". Familiar—or once familiar tactics on Cecil's part. He had had a masterly knack of denigrating a rival or an opponent, I remembered. He had never used it on me before, though.

166

Why should he feel the necessity to down-point me now, as if, in some way, I was a menace to him?

A pleasant night? It was more than that. It was a lovely night, windless and warm and heavy with flower scents; a night made for lovers.

"On such a night as this . . ." I quoted dreamily, as we paced up the drive, side by side, but not touching. Then, in the gathering dusk, I felt my skin burning. I hadn't intended the quotation as an incitement . . .

Mercifully for me, he didn't appear to recognise the quotation. He asked, almost pettishly: "Why did you have to come back here? Rather inconsistent, aren't you?"

"Inconsistent? No," I said, consideringly. "Anything but, I would have thought. 'Constant by name and Constant by nature', Angela used to call me. Remember?"

"Constant? To what? You were eager enough to get away from the village, after your father died."

"Oh, no! Not I. It was Belle who

insisted on our moving down to Devon to be near her. I suppose she had a conscience about Mother and salved it by keeping an eye on her."

"You could have come back when your mother died."

"Could I?" I asked doubtfully. "I had to find a job."

"You would have been welcomed back at St. Cyriac's."

"Possibly, but . . . what's all this in aid of, Cecil? Surely it's of no importance?"

"It's puzzling. Why you should choose to crash back into our lives just now," he said moodily. "A most inopportune moment. Mother should have realised that."

"Inopportune?" I echoed. "Why?"

"Because of Katy—and Aylward. He'll be out of hospital next week. How's he going to react to your presence?"

"Not unfavourably. Why should he? We were always good friends," I said defensively.

"What's Katy going to make of your good friendship? The poor kid's near the limit of her endurance. If she's goaded much further, something drastic will happen."

"You think she has suicidal tendencies? So does your mother. I don't. Katy wants to love and be loved . . . to matter tremendously to someone . . . for herself, not for her father's money or influence," I said, thinking aloud. "I can't believe that she and Aylward are a team. Could he have forgotten her, if she'd been all that important to him?"

"You haven't outgrown your romantic, idealistic notions, I perceive," Cecil said curtly. "Come down to earth! Hasn't it occurred to you that no one in this family can afford to indulge in such notions?"

"You can't afford to fall in love? Is that what you're implying? What a mundane outlook!"

"One has to be practical. Angela's doing pretty well at present, but her kind of popularity can be as ephemeral as Aylward's. Keep him away from the box for a few months—and who'll remember him?" Cecil said irritably. "The world of entertainment is a cut-throat, exacting and precarious form of rat-race. There's no real security in it."

"Well, your job is secure enough."

"Granted, but it's not as rewarding, financially, as laymen imagine. One's expenses are high, and steadily rising."

We were out of sight of the Lodge now, but not yet within sight of the Hall. A sharp bend hid us from both directions. Cecil halted and turned to me with a wry gesture.

"Why couldn't you have left me in peace? Why did you come back to tempt and tantalise me?" he demanded savagely.

"But . . . I didn't. I didn't suppose that I could," I said confusedly. "I thought you'd forgotten me."

"I thought I had." He gripped my wrists in a fierce, angry clasp. "Can't you see that I simply can't afford to remember you? To let myself care for you again? Have you no idea how much I loathe being hard-up—as we have been ever since Father left his affairs in a hopeless muddle?"

"Poverty is a question of degree; of proportion," I said tritely. "You've all three been earning more than I ever could —or Belle, either, in spite of her qualifications."

170

"It's different for girls in your position. Nobody expects you to make a splash. Or, if one was content to live and die as a hard-working country GP, one might not worry."

"That's not enough for you . . ."

"Why should it be? I have brains—and ambition. Why shouldn't I become a top-flight consultant?"

"No reason at all."

"Oh, yes, there is! Money and social status and influence still count. Who gets to the top of the ladder by merit alone? Precious few. Try to see it from my point of view, Conker. Having been born one of the Decointres of De Cointreaux Hall, why should I let myself sink into an obscure groove?"

"No reason at all," I repeated, wincing as his fingers clawed into my skin. "Why are you angry with me? I'm not trying to hinder you. Let go! You're hurting me . . ."

"I'd like to hurt you . . . to shake you and beat you. I've never wanted any other girl in the way I want you . . . but I'll be hanged if I'll let you shatter all my plans."

This was a facet of him which I had

barely glimpsed before. It wasn't a pleasing facet. I wrenched my hands free, in an involuntary movement of recoil.

"You don't have to eye me as if I were playing Delilah," I snapped. "What makes you imagine that I've the remotest interest in you now?"

"It's obvious. You wouldn't have grabbed at that job if it hadn't been with us. Angela always prophesied that we hadn't seen the last of you. She said you were terribly persistent, even as a kid," he retorted bluntly. "Angela'll be mad enough to murder you, if she thinks you're going to mess up her schemes for annexing the Haylett millions."

"You're very flattering. I had no idea that I was regarded as such an important and potentially dangerous person by your family circle."

"Don't make a joke of it! You had tremendous drawing power when you were a youngster. It's much more of a menace now that you're older and conscious of your own attractions."

"You're serious," I said incredulously. "You didn't talk that way when we were engaged."

"It would have been a pity to have spoilt your delightful unselfconsciousness. You were as open and trusting as a child."

"Yes."

I didn't add: "I trusted *you* . . ." but colour suddenly suffused his rather sallow skin.

"Don't make things harder for me, Conker. I can understand why you felt compelled to come here, but you must realise that it wouldn't work. When we had to let the Hall, we vowed that we'd get it back some day," he said slowly. "That should be Aylward's job, but one can't rely on him. If he doesn't soon pull himself together, Katy will find a counter-attraction."

"*Don't*! Put like that, it sounds hatefully cold-blooded . . . and not at all like Aylward."

"Still the sweet little romantic? Easy to pretend to be shocked at the notion of marrying money, but, if you had the chance to play Cinderella, wouldn't you jump at it? You know you would," he said cynically.

I shook my head. I turned. Futile to

prolong this session. What else had we to say to each other?

Instantly, his hands reached out for me again. This time, he grabbed at my arms and swung me round to face him. Then, he was kissing me . . . not in the old, light, easy, comradely fashion, but with a savagery and a passion which seemed equally incongruous to his old and to his new image. It was the kind of embrace which, described in a romance, was calculated to give the reader a vicarious thrill. I had never experienced anything like it before. I was dismayed and disappointed that, instead of "quickening my heartbeats", and "sweeping away all my qualms", and "overcoming my resistance", or "transporting me to the seventh heaven", Cecil was making it difficult for me to breathe and straining my back muscles.

I felt awkward and embarrassed and far from "with it". It was as if I had been thrust on to a stage without any preliminary rehearsals, without indeed even knowing what play was being performed.

His breath was hot on my face, but his hands felt cold through the thin material of my green dress. The air was colder now that darkness was approaching. It was still only May . . . reputedly the most treacherous of months. I should have put on a coat, I thought regretfully. Or . . . I should have refused to "take a stroll". Only, how could I have foreseen this?

I wriggled. I squirmed. I didn't want to offend his touchy pride . . . but I should have a stiff neck and a stiff back tomorrow if I was held at this angle much longer. In sheer desperation, I let myself go limp, sagging at the knees, as if I was about to collapse in what a Victorian novelist might have called a "maidenly swoon".

Mercifully, it worked more effectively than a hack on the shins—the one alternative I'd had in mind—and without apparently causing offence.

"Here, steady! Brace up, Conker!" Cecil ejaculated in alarm. "What's the matter?"

I didn't answer. Eyes tightly closed, I sagged against him. He gave me a slight, impatient shake. I let my head fall back against his shoulder and uttered a soft moan.

"Look here—" He sounded as flustered as a nervous medical student coping with his first casualty. "Brace up, silly! I didn't hurt you . . ."

Suddenly afraid that, in his panic, he might deposit me on the grass verge of the drive, with subsequent damage to my best frock, I sighed and blinked up at him.

"I—I felt queer . . ." I said faintly.

"Sorry, but it was no more than you deserved," he said irritably. "You were asking for it. You ought to have had more sense than to crash in on us again."

"Yes," I said weakly. "One hasn't really any reverse gear, emotionally. One can't put back a clock in one's life. A 'time machine', to transport people back into the past, wouldn't be a paying proposition once it had lost its novelty. People would find the past exceedingly uncomfortable."

"Here, pull yourself together! You sound light-headed," Cecil said concernedly. "Lean on me, and let's get back to the house."

"I'm OK now, thanks." I drew away from him and tried to smooth my hair. "You had some instructions to give me about my patient—or so you said."

He frowned and cleared his throat. Even

in the fading light, I could see that he looked several degrees less sure of himself.

"Is she your patient, too?" I asked. "How come?"

"Not officially. Oh, no! I've merely tried to keep a brotherly eye on her since she was discharged from hospital," he explained. "She hasn't seen her own family doctor since she flounced out of her father's house and took refuge with Mother. It was embarrassing for us, but we could scarcely send her back, especially as her father was just off to the West Indies. Katy's in no state to be left alone. Heaven knows what she might or might not do!"

"You suggested that she needed a nurse?"

"The responsibility was too much for Mother. If anything were to happen to that idiot child, her father wouldn't hesitate to blame us. Now . . ." His frown deepened. "You do realise what you've let yourself in for, I hope?"

"To some extent, yes."

"And the prospect doesn't alarm you?"

"I haven't seen any evidence yet of suicidal tendencies," I answered bluntly.

"Or of any imbecility. Katy's had a bad shock, and she's worried and unhappy about Aylward. In herself, she seems normal enough to me. Basically, that is."

"It's not a well-balanced, stable personality. With her background and upbringing, one can't expect much common sense or grasp of reality."

"She's not the traditional 'spoilt brat'. Far from it," I protested. "I would call her 'deprived'. Hence her yearning for a happy family life."

"Probably you haven't had sufficient experience to recognise dangerous symptoms. I can only warn you to take every precaution," he said grimly.

It was true that I hadn't come into contact with mentally disturbed cases; "nut-cases", as they were commonly called. Yet, wouldn't the very fact that I was used to dealing with normal people have alerted some sixth sense in me, had my newest patient been abnormal in any way?

I tried, falteringly, to voice that opinion, but Cecil stamped on it with both neatly shod feet. He appeared to be convinced that Katy was a potential suicide. He gave me enough warnings to have turned my hair grey, had I taken them as seriously as he intended them.

I mustn't let Katy go near the edge of a cliff or any steep steps. I mustn't let her sleep with a wide-open window. I mustn't let her drive the Cortina. I must keep all drugs—even aspirin—safely under lock and key. I mustn't leave her alone in a house where there was gas. I mustn't allow her to secrete any sharp knives or razor blades. In fact, I had better remove her scissors—if she had any . . .

"This is fantastic," I protested, before he'd finished. "Granted that she might want to injure herself—and I can't see any signs of it—she wouldn't consider such a diversity of methods. Nobody would. The kind of woman who would stick her neck in a gas oven would never dream of hurling herself over a precipice—and vice versa. I can't picture Katy's going in for violence or anything painful or disfiguring."

"You can't?"

"Certainly not. If she had any self-destructive impulse, she would get herself up attractively, take enough aspirin to put her out, and arrange herself gracefully on her bed, praying fervently that she would be found before it was too late," I assured him. "It would be one of those childish— 'I'll make them sorry they weren't nicer to me'—acts."

There was a brief pause. Then, he said unsmilingly: "You've changed. You used not to be so sure of yourself and your opinions. You were much more malleable."

"Five years ago? I can't remember that I was ever given much chance to voice my opinions. At St. Cyriac's, I was merely a second-year student nurse. At home, after Father died, Belle made all the decisions. Before that, in our early days, we were swept along in Angela's wake," I recalled. "For the past three years I've been independent. Miss Henrietta taught me to think for myself."

He made a dissatisfied sound, akin to a grunt, and I sighed.

The end of a dream, I thought, as we walked back to the Lodge in silence. Not with a clean-cut razor-blade slash: not with one gloriously fierce explosion, like a rocket on Guy Fawkes' night, but with a sigh and a grunt.

"That was brief, for a romantic reunion," Katy said meaningly, as I scurried upstairs to my room, with her hard on my heels like an eager puppy. "Was it a thrill? Did he clasp you to him?"

"No thrill," I said regretfully. "Just mutual disappointment."

"He kissed you. Look at your hair and your smudged lipstick," she said, leaning over my shoulder to survey my reflection in the wardrobe mirror, before which I had halted. "You're pale, though; not blushing prettily."

"I'm all wrong for him now. He wants someone naïve and adoring and malleable, with money and a good social background, to help him up the ladder."

"But . . . he kissed you," she reiterated hopefully.

"What's a kiss? Not a pledge of undying devotion. Men kiss you 'Hello!' and they kiss you 'Goodbye!'" I swung round and caught the dismay in her eyes. "Oh, Katy, don't tell me that you've been building a whole future on a few stray kisses?"

"As Angela said, Aylward isn't a cad.

He wouldn't kiss a girl unless he really loved her."

"A man doesn't have to be a cad—what a deliciously old-world term!—to kiss a girl as pretty as you. The way you look and act, you're asking to be kissed and hugged."

Her expressive eyes widened, as if I had startled and shocked her. I suddenly felt years older than my age.

"You'd better go down and say goodbye to Cecil," I said, moving over to the dressing-table.

"Aren't you coming down again?"

"Presently. It doesn't need three of us to see Cecil to his car."

11

"The hope I dreamed of was a dream
Was but a dream; and now I wake."
CHRISTINA G. ROSSETTI

"IS this the place? It's terribly lonely. You lived here for three years? Oh, how could you endure it?" Katy exclaimed, with an exaggerated shiver.

It was a fine, sunny evening, but a brisk breeze was blowing in from the Atlantic. The cottage stood high up on the rugged cliffs above the small, in-curved cove. As we walked up the flagged path, from the garage to the front door, the wind seemed to rush at us in a chilly embrace.

I breathed the cold salt air in gratefully. It was like a tonic after all the dust and the reek of petrol and diesel on the roads. Seabirds were whirling and mewling overhead. From behind the front door came a volley of excited barking.

"I love it," I said frankly. "I was never

183

lonely here. I was much lonelier in Plymouth after Mother died."

"Whatever did you find to do when you were off duty?"

"Plenty. There's a good riding stables quite near. I rode a lot. In the summer, I bathed. I had the use of the car. I could roam where I pleased. I'm a country girl. Remember?"

Martha must have heard the car. The front door swung open—and Berry came out like a rocket, to hurl himself at me. His lithe, wriggling brown body was dancing and leaping around my ankles, tail thumping madly, velvety muzzle nuzzling me. I bent down and scooped him up into my arms. He whimpered ecstatically and tried to lick me all over.

"That dog! He's been fair miserable without you, Nurse," Martha greeted me, as I carried Berry up the steps. "Wouldn't eat, and howled like a banshee."

"Oh, dear!" I said in dismay. "If I'd known . . ."

"Couldn't get in touch with you, seeing that you didn't leave any telephone number . . . and you didn't think to ring up," she said reproachfully. "If I hadn't got your telegram yesterday, I'd have had to ask the vet to take the dog, before he drove me round the bend."

"I'm sorry. I didn't guess he would fret. He always seemed such a happy little fellow," I said remorsefully. "Berry, pet, I'm sorry, but you're my boy now, and I won't leave you again."

"It was only natural. It may have been Miss Henrietta who bought him, but you've been caring for him since he was a pup," Martha reminded me. "Come you in out of the cold wind! Kettle's on the boil, and there's a good fire in the sitting-room."

I introduced Katy, and old Martha said ruefully: "Our loss is your gain, as they say. It isn't only the dog that's been missing Nurse. You'd be surprised how many folk in the village have been asking after her and wanting to know when she'll be back. She has a way with her . . . and there's no denying it. I've been missing her, come to that. 'She lightens up the house', as my Miss Henrietta used to say."

"Did she? How sweet of her! I suppose she was thinking of my hair," I said hurriedly. "You've been all right, haven't you, Martha? You haven't been nervous at night?"

"It's been kind of lonesome. I'm thinking it won't be so good come the autumn and winter," Martha admitted. "Maybe I should look out for a paying guest or two."

She had laid on a sumptuous "high tea" for us. I was pleased to see that Katy ate smoke-cured ham and eggs and fresh salad, Cornish splits, with Cornish cream and home-made raspberry jam, and a slice of gooseberry pie with schoolgirlish relish.

After we'd toasted ourselves by the blazing log fire, we took Berry out for a brief run. There wasn't much wrong with Katy physically, I thought, as we scrambled down the narrow, winding path to the cove, and ran over the sands, with Berry cavorting excitedly around us. She was "sound in wind and limb", as we used to say of our ponies. It was only when she began to brood over her fall and Aylward's amnesia that she waxed hysterical. Basically, she was no more neurotic than any other girl of eighteen whose romance was perilously near the rocks.

She didn't need the careful watching

which Cecil had advised. What she needed was distraction . . . not to be given time to dwell on her own problems. Finding sticks and throwing them for Berry to retrieve, she might have been eight years old. She had a lovely colour and her eyes were shining like sapphires when we turned back to the cliff path. She really was enchantingly pretty; at least, when she was happy, I decided—and Dr. Alistair McCanning appeared to agree with me.

"That raw-boned, red-headed Scot", as Everton Gillard called him, was waiting in the sitting-room when we regained the cottage. Berry rushed in on him, barking a welcome, before we had a chance to dash upstairs and tidy ourselves.

"Heard you were expected back tonight, Connie, so I thought I'd just look in and find out how you'd fared in the great metropolis," Alistair proclaimed, with an attempt at jauntiness—but his eyes were fixed on Katy as if on a vision.

I was smiling inwardly as I performed the introduction, because Katy was eyeing the young doctor with unconcealed interest—and he was more than reciprocating it.

187

"Haylett?" he echoed. "That's an uncommon name . . . except in connection with frozen foods."

"That's my father. The frozen-food merchant, I mean," Katy answered naïvely.

"Is that so?" He glanced inquiringly from Katy to me. "You've never mentioned that you were on visiting terms with the Hayletts, Connie."

"I'm not. I've never met Mr. Haylett. Miss Haylett was involved in a nasty climbing accident quite recently. I'm looking after her while she's convalescing," I explained.

Berry was nosing my ankles and making whimpering noises. I picked him up and stroked him.

"Hungry, fellow? I'll get you some dinner . . ."

I turned to ask Alistair to excuse me, but Katy had begun to tell him all about her fall, and he was listening absorbedly, so I retreated in silence.

After his self-imposed fast, the dachshund was ravenously hungry. He made short work of a tin of dog food and a handful of dog meal.

"Some earnest young vet might have called you 'neurotic', while I was away, if not suicidal," I told him. "You and Katy are a pair. . . highly strung and determined to have your own way, but perfectly normal in your reactions. Show you a pretty little dachshund bitch, or show Katy a personable young bachelor, and you'll both forget your troubles."

Berry looked up at me with velvety, meltingly eloquent brown eyes, as if to assure me that in no circumstances would he ever forget me.

"He's what they call a one-man dog, and that's plain," Martha observed, from the rocking-chair beside the kitchen stove. "He'll never have any use for anyone else."

Luckily, that didn't apply to Katy, I thought hopefully. Katy might be convinced that Aylward was the only man in the world for her . . . but how many other attractive men had she met? She had turned involuntarily towards Alistair as a flower starved of light and warmth turns towards the sun. Natural and inevitable, one might have reasoned. Then . . . why wasn't it that way with *me*? Why couldn't

I respond to Alistair . . . or to Everton Gillard?

I looked at Martha, the picture of contentment, rocking gently in the old chair, her feet in comfortable slippers extended towards the stove, one plump cat curled up on her lap, and two asleep on the rug at her feet. Her wrinkled but still rosy face wore an expression of gentle serenity. She was safe in harbour; safe from stormy seas. For three years, I had shared that harbour with her. Now I had sailed out of it, but to what port was I heading?

Almost startling in its shrillness, the telephone bell suddenly shattered the silence.

"For Dr. McCanning, I expect," I said. "I'll answer it."

The telephone was in the second, smaller sitting-room which Miss Henrietta had used as her working room. I ran down the passage to it, with Berry at my heels, playfully pawing at my ankles.

"Don't, silly! You'll trip me up. Stop it!" I panted, and reached the telephone just as the bell stopped pealing.

To my surprise, it was the operator who

answered my "Hello!" and inquired if I was Port Mathers 267. A long-distance call, I thought in sudden anxiety. From whom? Mary Decointre, worried about Katy? Who else knew that I would be here this evening? Had I told Everton? I had told Cecil. Perhaps he had some more urgent warnings to give me. Odd that the prospect of hearing Cecil's voice should be vaguely irritating rather than exhilarating. Odd—and saddening. Did nothing last in this world? I wouldn't have believed that there could ever be a time when I would rather not hear from Cecil . . .

The operator called: "You're through. Go ahead . . ." and I braced myself.

"Hello! Hello!" I repeated edgily. "Port Mathers 267."

"Conker? What's wrong? You sound a mite distrait. Have I interrupted something?"

Even over all those miles of wires, the soft, familiar drawl was unmistakable. The blood seemed to rush up to my temples.

"Aylward? It's *you*? No. No, of course not. I'm just breathless," I stammered. "I was in the kitchen, feeding the dog. How —how are you?"

"Fine, thanks, but mighty bored here. Brother Cecil looked in this afternoon, and told me you'd gone back to Cornwall. Not for long, I hope?"

"Oh, no! We'll be back in Netherfield Green for your homecoming. How did you get hold of this number?"

"Via my mamma. I guessed you'd leave it with her. I wanted to make sure that you'd arrived safely . . . and that you were coming back."

"Well, thank you . . ." I said awkwardly—and heard him chuckle.

"No thanks necessary. Pure self-indulgence. I had a yearning to hear your voice, my love . . . to make sure that I hadn't been dreaming again."

"Oh! Have you been dreaming a lot? Having nightmares?" I asked confusedly.

"Waking and sleeping. I'm in the most hopeless muddle. I hardly know whether I'm going or coming, as old Mrs. Mussett used to say. Remember her?"

"The old cook at the Hall? Oh, yes! She was a sweetie. Of course, I remember her, and the hand-outs she gave us at the kitchen door when we were starving after a long trek. She could always produce

192

apples and carrots and lumps of sugar for the ponies, too."

"You've a good memory, Conker."

"Too good, I've thought some-times . . ."

"'Memories that bless and burn'? Remember the blessings and try to forget the burns."

"I do, but . . . things . . . and people change. The changes tend to blur one's memories."

"You haven't changed—and neither have I. Some things remain as constant as the sun. What has been, *is*—and will be. That's not a dream or a delusion, is it? Where we're concerned, I mean?"

There was something beneath his light, easy drawl; something which I found profoundly disturbing. It was akin to an SOS; an unvoiced appeal for help.

"I could never change towards *you*," I said impulsively. "Aylward, tell me what's wrong. You're worried, aren't you?"

"Who wouldn't be—in my position? I'm being asked to swallow facts—or fancies—which stick in my throat," he answered ruefully. "Could I have acted right out of character? Could I have been more than slightly crazy without suspecting it?"

"Certainly not. You've always been very well balanced."

"I suppose I could have had a sudden brain-storm. That's what brother Cecil appears to think. But . . . can I be held responsible for it now? Am I bound by anything I may have said or done when I wasn't fully conscious?"

"Certainly not," I said again, firmly. "Don't listen to Cecil—or to anyone else. Don't let yourself be pushed into anything that doesn't appeal to you. If you'd like to take a job as Warden on a nature reserve, go ahead. It's your life."

"Bless you for those kind words, my love!"

There was suddenly a confused murmur of voices . . . and then Aylward's again: "I'm being forcibly removed from the telephone and marched off to bed, so I'll say good night, love . . . 'parting is such sweet sorrow' . . ."

The line went dead. I was smiling as I put down the receiver. Darling Aylward! He had always been ready to champion me in the old days, and to fight my battles for me. Would-be humorists in the school playground, who had called me "Smithy", and pretended to warm their hands on my hair, hadn't done it twice. Now it was my turn to champion him. If he would rather be a Warden than a "TV personality", why not? Why should he be expected to devote himself to an uncongenial job for the sake of that impractical old house?

Yes, but the Decanters weren't expecting Aylward to work for the Hall, but to marry for it. With an acute sense of guilt, I remembered that neither I nor Aylward had even mentioned Katy. I had yielded to my impulse to comfort and reassure him. I ought to have reminded myself that Katy was in equal need of comfort . . . and I was supposed to be looking after her.

The kitchen door opened, and Martha emerged with a tray.

"I've made you a fresh pot of tea, and there's some of my biscuits with it. Best you should have a cup now and get off to bed," she advised me. "Young missy looks as if she needs her sleep. Kind of peaky and overstrung."

"She isn't very strong," I said, feeling

guilty again. "Thank you, Martha. Shall I take the tray?"

Katy's blue eyes were still bright, but there were smudges under them, which Alistair had obviously noticed.

"You need building up, m'lass," he told Katy. "If I were your doctor, I'd prescribe a long holiday here, relaxing in the sea air, with Martha's good cooking to put some meat on your bones."

Katy made a laughing grimace and asked if he would like to turn her into a "buxom country wench"?

"Why not? Who wants to hug a bag of skin and bones?" he retorted.

"You're fearfully rude," Katy rebuked him, but, after he had left us, she said wistfully: "I wish he were my doctor."

"Do you? Behind that brusque manner, he can be very kind. The villagers think no end of him."

"Are you going to marry him?" she asked directly.

"I shouldn't imagine so. He hasn't proposed to me, anyway."

"Oh, but men don't, nowadays, go all formal about it!" Katy said quickly. "They're much more casual."

"If a man wanted me to marry him, I would expect him to say so, loud and clear."

"A young man wouldn't. He'd just grab you and kiss you—and you would know that was it," she persisted.

It was on the tip of my tongue to ask: "Surely Aylward mentioned marriage?" but she yawned and said: "Gosh, I'm sleepy!"

With Alistair's departure, her colour and animation had gone, too. She was looking pale and curiously forlorn.

"Bed for you, my lass!" I said firmly, and she smiled wanly.

"That's what your doctor friend called me. It must be catching."

12

"Life, and the world, and mine own self
are changed
For a dream's sake."

CHRISTINA G. ROSSETTI

"KATY—" with a sudden sense of urgency, I bent over the bed, seized Katy by her shoulders and shook her. "Katy, wake up, will you? Katy . . ."

She mumbled something, but she didn't open her eyes. She was breathing heavily . . . too heavily. I glanced at the bedside table distractedly. A small bottle of capsules stood on it beside a half-empty glass of water. The capsules hadn't been there last night when I had seen Katy to bed.

I snatched up the bottle. The label had been torn off, and the parti-coloured capsules inside might have been any kind of drug. Where, when and from whom had Katy obtained those capsules? The bottle

198

must have been carefully concealed among her belongings. Certainly, I hadn't seen it before.

She didn't appear to be in distress—or in a coma; just fathoms deep in sleep; the kind of sleep induced by drink or drugs. She might surface naturally in her own time . . . but she might not. I couldn't afford to take a chance.

I ran downstairs to the telephone, trying to banish the echo of Cecil's grave, warning voice from my ears. My fingers were trembling as I dialled Alistair's number.

"Hello! You're around bright and early. It's not eight o'clock yet," he said reproachfully, in response to my: "Alistair? It's Constant Smith here . . ."

"I know, and I suppose you're having breakfast, but could you please come over here at once," I said breathlessly.

"I haven't had a mouthful yet," he answered in his literal fashion. "What's the urgency?"

"It's Katy. She's taken some sleeping pills or something. I can't wake her."

"What has she taken and how many?"

"That's just what I don't know—and why I'm worried. They may have been quite mild, but they've certainly knocked her out," I said, trying to speak calmly. "I think you should have a look at her. To be on the safe side."

"Right! I'll be with you shortly. Don't panic!"

I wasn't in a panic. I was simply puzzled and worried. That was only natural, I thought crossly, as I put down the receiver. What had prompted Katy to get up again and swallow those capsules, after I had settled her down for the night? She must have moved around very quietly, or she would have alerted me. She was sleeping in what had been Miss Henrietta's room, and I was next door. There wasn't a communicating door, but I had left my door to the landing ajar. Had Katy called out, I should have heard her. I had always heard Miss Henrietta's calls.

I looked in on Katy, but she hadn't moved. I retreated to my own room, and dressed hurriedly. I swallowed down another cup of tea from the pot Martha had brought us. Berry, who had spent the night sprawled out luxuriously at the end of my bed, stretched and yawned and blinked at me. I patted his sleek head absently.

"I should have been a veterinary surgeon's nurse-assistant," I said aloud. "People are too complicated and too unpredictable for me. I'd thought Katy was in good spirits last night."

I felt ruffled and guilty. I had flattered myself that I understood Katy and had been accepted by her as a friend. Evidently, I had been wrong, or she wouldn't have put this over on me.

What could have been her motive? She couldn't have been afraid that she would have a sleepless night. She had been half asleep already when I had seen her into bed. Or . . . had that been an act?

It was a blessed relief to pour out my fears to Alistair when he reached the cottage, five minutes later.

"I didn't—and I still can't believe that she has this suicidal tendency . . . but what else could have prompted her to take a hefty dose of sleeping pills last night when she obviously didn't need it?" I finished in exasperation.

He patted me reassuringly on the shoulder.

"Not to worry. I'll ask her," he said, in the tone of one who intended to be answered. "It's dangerous to fool around with any kind of drug. One can go too far —and I doubt me if that was the lassie's intention. A bid for attention, more likely."

When he had examined Katy and the remaining capsules in the unlabelled bottle, his reaction was a reflection of my own, except that his was devoid of that shadow of guilt. Katy, in his opinion, had taken a double dose rather than an over-dose, of what he suspected to be nembutal. A pointless proceeding, as far as Alistair could see, and potentially dangerous, he pronounced, with a fine roll of the "r". She was in no immediate danger, phys-ically, but she did appear to be danger-ously irresponsible. She needed to be spoken to severely.

"Go right ahead!" I said, feeling that I could hug him. He was uncompromisingly honest and normal and practical. No dark hints from Alistair. He would always speak his mind. "Perhaps she'll listen to you . . .

a stranger. She said last night that she wished you were her doctor."

"Did she now?" He looked boyishly gratified, but instantly compressed his features into a stern expression. "The poor wee lassie! One of those mixed-up, over-indulged, undisciplined youngsters? Secretly yearning to be taken in hand?"

"Not exactly. Neglected, I fancy. Emotionally, anyway."

I repeated what Katy had told me about her father, and he nodded absently.

"This boy she plans to marry?" he said inquiringly. "Too soft with her, is he?"

"He isn't a boy. Probably more of a father image to her . . . her father, that is. Popular and charming," I said confusedly. "Can you give her something to rouse her? Or do we leave her to sleep off whatever the dope is?"

"We could, but I reckon we should play it her way—to get at what's in her mind," Alistair said grimly. "The lassie's expecting to have caused alarm and dismay. It's plain she intended to frighten you. She'll be gratified to find a medical man in attendance, working on her—and ready to explain herself, or I'll know the reason why not . . ."

He looked and sounded surprisingly formidable—and years older than his age. I began to realise why the country people respected as well as liked him. He might be impatient with any form of malingering, too outspoken for some patients' taste—but in any emergency he could be completely reliable. He would never acquire Cecil's bedside manner or Cecil's sleek air of prosperity, but I doubted if he shared Cecil's ambitions. Probably, Alistair would stay on here, his practice steadily increasing, till he became a local legend.

"Go and make a pot of strong black coffee. I've a surgery at nine-thirty, so I'd better get to grips with the lassie," he said, gazing down at Katy with a mixture of displeasure and compassion. "I'll be talking to her like a father."

"As her own father doesn't," I murmured, and left him to it.

As I had warned Katy, my reactions weren't those of the orthodox trained nurse. Instead of hurrying back upstairs, I lingered in the kitchen, and tried to explain the situation to Martha, who had been alarmed by Alistair's early visit.

My version—that Katy had taken too many tablets by mistake—caused Martha to shake her greying head understandingly and observe: "It'll be a man, I don't doubt. It always is, at her age. Ah, there are compensations in growing old, Nurse! No more heartaches . . ."

She spoke so feelingly that I was conscious of a twinge of compunction. Dear Martha was one of those dependable, background people whom one tended to take for granted. I had never thought of her as the young girl she had been, in the years before she had come to live with Miss Henrietta. Had she suffered—and survived—some ill-fated love affairs?

"Poor young thing!" she said, after a pause. "She'll learn, but it's sometimes a painful lesson that you can love without being loved."

"It is, indeed," I agreed.

The percolator was bubbling over and filling the kitchen with the tang of sizzling coffee. Reluctantly, I put it on a tray with cream, sugar, and three cups, and headed upstairs again.

Katy was sitting up in bed, her dressing-gown wrapped round her shoulders. Her fair hair was in a wild disorder, her face was flushed, and there was the glint of tears in her eyes. She looked like a small girl who had been slapped and sent to bed for some misdemeanour.

"Angela? And who is this Angela that you should take her word for gospel truth?" Alistair was demanding, in a growling voice, his "r's" very much in evidence. "Can you not think for yourself, my lassie?"

"She's his twin sister. She knows him better than I do. She was sure it would work," Katy said defensively. "She promised that they wouldn't hurt me. Two or three, she said, but I only took two . . ."

"Angela?" I echoed, setting the tray down with a clatter. "Are you saying that Angela gave you those capsules?"

She nodded, her expression turning sulky.

"Angela said to use them if Aylward was difficult . . . to give him a fright."

"But . . . why take them last night when Aylward's miles away?" I demanded.

206

Her colour deepened. She looked down at her clasped hands in sullen silence.

"To frighten me?" I said incredulously. "Why? What have I done?"

There was no answer. Impatiently, Alistair gestured to me to pour out the coffee. He took the first cup from me, added cream and a liberal helping of sugar, and bent over the bed.

"Drink this, my lass. It'll pull you together," he said in a gentler tone. Then, over his shoulder, he answered my question with a curt: "Apparently, it's what you didn't do, Nurse."

"Oh?" I said, perplexed and somewhat chilled by that curt, crisp "Nurse". "What did I omit?"

"Something in connection with a telephone call," he answered for Katy. "We heard the bell peal last evening. I supposed the call was for me, and I opened the door to take it . . . but you were already there . . . so I closed the door again."

"You didn't see or hear us. You were much too deeply absorbed." Katy jerked up her chin and glowered at me. "You didn't call me. You didn't even tell me afterwards . . . but I knew. I knew you were talking to Aylward."

To my vexation, I felt my cheeks burning. The accusation in her tone—and to a lesser degree in Alistair's—was unmistakable. So was the inference Katy had drawn from my reticence. I bit my lips. What convincing retort could I make?

"Well?" she challenged me triumphantly. "You can't deny it, can you?"

I shook my head. Automatically, I turned to the tray again and poured out coffee for myself and Alistair.

"There was no good reason for telling you," I said, after another pause.

"No reason? When my fiancé rings up to talk to me, there's no reason to call me?" Katy cried out indignantly.

"He didn't," I said flatly. "He didn't ask for you. He didn't even mention you. I'm sorry if that hurts. It's mainly why I didn't speak of his call."

"Is that true?" The colour began to ebb from her cheeks and tears to well up in her eyes. "He still hasn't remembered me? And yet he remembers *you*? Oh, I can't bear it!"

"I'm sorry," I repeated awkwardly.

208

"Truly, I'm sorry on your account, Katy. Perhaps it's as Cecil suggested, and Aylward's subconscious is deliberately escaping into the past because it's loth to face the future."

"The future? Our future? Oh, how can you be so cruel? Cecil didn't say that," she protested tearfully.

"Not with regard to you, of course," I explained hurriedly. "Cecil thinks Aylward is reluctant to shoulder his family responsibilities—or perhaps the responsibilities of his television work. If you've the wrong temperament for it, to appear before all those cameras and a huge, unseen audience must be a ghastly strain. I should detest it."

"Would you? I thought it was fun . . . the bit we filmed before my accident," she said ingenuously. "Angela told me that I was wonderfully photogenic. I don't suppose you are."

"Who cares?" I retorted irritably. "Don't you realise how foolish it was to take drugs which hadn't been prescribed for you? Foolish and dangerous. You could have put yourself out for good."

"So he was saying . . ." Katy shot a

thoughtful side-glance at Alistair. "Would it have mattered much? Not to Aylward, if he has forgotten me—and who else is there to care what happens to me?"

"That's no way for a young lassie to talk," Alistair said severely, but his eyes were kinder than his tone.

"You don't understand how alone I am," Katy said, in a forlorn "little girl" voice. "I did think Angela and Mrs. Decointre cared about me . . . but it's just Father's money . . ."

Alistair made a kind of growling sound and called for another cup of coffee for her. He swallowed the coffee I had poured out for him, hurriedly and abstractedly, then announced that he must get along to his surgery.

"You will look in again?" Katy's moist, appealing eyes really did look remarkably like water forget-me-nots. That sapphire-like sparkle was absent. Her whole manner was forlorn and subdued. I wondered if she were putting on an act for Alistair's benefit or if she really had had a fright.

Alistair was decidedly curt with me when I escorted him downstairs.

"I'll look in tonight, after surgery," he

said shortly. "Get her to take things easily for the next day or two."

"We're supposed to be going back to Netherfield Green tomorrow."

"Out of the question! The lassie needs to relax, not to be rushed around. She's had a bad shock," he pronounced.

"Yes, but that was some time ago now," I protested. "At her age . . ."

"At her age, one can be pitifully vulnerable." He gave me a censorious glance. "Couldn't you have left her sweetheart to her? You gave her an unpleasant shock yesterday evening."

He didn't say: "You should be ashamed of yourself—" but he looked it, and I felt my colour rising—in indignation rather than guiltiness.

"We're very old friends, Aylward and I. Nothing more. I hadn't seen him for five years till I went to the hospital with Katy. Can I help it if he remembered me?"

I had meant to speak coolly and reasonably, but my voice betrayed me. Why must both he and Katy leap to such an erroneous and unfair conclusion?

Alistair shook his head grimly.

"That horse is a non-runner. We heard

the tone of your voice when you were talking to him. I didn't know then who was on the line, but I recognised instantly that he was the man in your life."

"That's nonsense! I've never thought of Aylward in that way . . ."

"No business of mine." He cut me short with an impatient gesture. "Except as it affects yon wee lassie. You'd better try to make your peace with her before she does something more drastic, which you'll both regret."

"Can't you see that she's merely play-acting? She hasn't any desire to kill herself."

"Granted, but she could go too far without intending to—as she might have done last night. Reckless showing off can be very dangerous, you ken."

"I ken that most men are fools when a girl is small and fair and feminine, with big, appealing blue eyes," I snapped. "I don't doubt that that's how Aylward got himself enmeshed. He's the chivalrous type, too."

He gave me a very chilly glance at that and stalked off down the flagged path to his weather-beaten looking estate car.

"Oh, think what you please! Who cares?" I breathed at his stiff, retreating back, but exasperation couldn't heal an acute sense of hurt.

For three years, Alistair and I had shared a pleasant, heartening friendship, which might in time have warmed into a lasting attachment. Now it was at an end. He would never again view me with the old, uncomplicated admiration and approval. There was a chasm between us nearly as formidable as the chasm between me and Cecil.

I told myself angrily that it was the sheer injustice of it which stung. Why should I be cast for the invidious rôle of "the other woman"? Simply because I refused to be disloyal to the past and my memories of those happy days when Aylward had been my hero?

"Life and the world and mine own self are changed. For a dream's sake . . ." flashed into my mind. Miss Henrietta had used that quotation in one of the novels I had typed for her. *For A Dream's Sake,* she had called the story . . .

Yes, but why should my world be changed around me "for a dream's sake"?

That was all Aylward would ever mean to me . . . a childish dream. It wasn't fair that I should be made to suffer for a dream.

13

"You will discover how much you care,
And will give your heart to a dog to tear."

RUDYARD KIPLING

IT wasn't until later in the morning, when I took a tray of tea and biscuits up to Katy's room for "elevenses", that I realised the secondary—or was it the primary?—reason for her "lost waif" look.

She asked with childish directness: "Do you think she planned to kill me?"

"What? Who?" For a moment, I couldn't follow her trend of thought. "To kill you?"

"Angela," she said flatly. "She gave me those tablets."

"Which was very wrong of her, or, at least, very foolish," I said tentatively.

"She could have hoped that they would 'put me out for good', as your nice doctor said. It would have been 'for good' where

Angela was concerned." Katy's voice quivered. "With my money, and what Aylward could earn, the family could go back to the Hall."

"Angela has her studios and her service flat in Town. She wouldn't want to live in Netherfield Green again."

"No, but she'd like her mother and brother to be living there." She looked at me defiantly. "I'll bet it was Angela who pushed me off that mountain path. Probably, Aylward saw her—and it shocked him so badly that he deliberately blotted out all memory of it."

"Don't let your imagination sweep you away with it!"

What else could I say? It wouldn't help to assure Katy that her suspicions were monstrous.

"I'm going to ring her up and ask her about those capsules," Katy announced resolutely. "You can't stop me."

"I wouldn't try. If there's a conspiracy against you, as you appear to imagine, I'm not in on it."

"Aren't you? But . . . mightn't that be why Mrs. Decointre seized on you?

Because you're not fully trained, and because she knew you would never give any of them away? You'd cover up for one of that family, no matter what."

"No." I shook my head. "I don't think so. After all this time, they wouldn't count on me. Even Angela couldn't expect to dominate me now, as if I were still a child. Besides, even a half-trained nurse puts her patient first."

There was no extension to Miss Henrietta's telephone, so, if I'd wanted to, I couldn't have listened in to Katy's call. She emerged from it looking ruffled and bewildered, and yet with a gleam of excitement in her expressive eyes.

"They're coming here. Angela's bringing Aylward down tomorrow," she announced. "She says not to worry if you haven't rooms for them. They'll find somewhere to stay."

"Aylward? He doesn't get out of hospital till Wednesday. He certainly isn't fit for a long drive," I protested.

"Angela says she'll fix it. She thinks the change of scene will do him good and jolt him into remembering."

"I should think that's highly unlikely.

To find himself in completely strange surroundings will leave him more at a loss than ever," I said irritably. "They can't stay here. There's only one vacant room— a small attic—and this isn't my house. The Fishermen's Repose in the village lets rooms, but they won't be very comfortable there."

"I did tell Angela that there weren't any spare bedrooms here, but you know what she is. Once she makes up her mind, one can't alter it for her."

"Heaven knows why she should have made up her mind to rush down here!" I said uneasily. "What's the point?"

"She talked about a change of scene and —and a romantic setting." Katy coloured self-consciously. "Perhaps she means Aylward to fall in love with me all over again."

"What did she say about those capsules?"

"Nothing much . . . except to insist that they couldn't have hurt me unless I'd swallowed half a dozen. She couldn't understand why you should have worked yourself into such a flap . . ." She paused, as if deliberately checking herself.

"Yes?" I said. "Go on! What else?"

Katy wriggled like a child confronting an irate adult.

"Oh, this and that! She doesn't like you, does she?"

"Doesn't she?" I wondered what Angela had said to give Katy that impression. "I wouldn't know. I've been out of touch with her for so long."

"Well—" Katy appeared to be bracing herself. "Angela hinted that you might have given me some dope . . . and hoped that her capsules would be held responsible . . ."

"For what? For your untimely death? How utterly ridiculous! You must have misunderstood her," I said incredulously. "I'm supposed to be looking after you. Why in the world should I want something disastrous to happen to you?"

"It was Angela's idea. Not mine." Her lower lip quivered like a hurt child's. "I took to you at once. I thought we were friends. Angela said I was a fool to trust you . . . but I don't trust her, either. It's pretty grim . . ."

"To have to suspect everyone in your circle of ulterior motives? It must be. You poor child!" I said, compassion over-coming exasperation. "Why don't you try using your own judgment? You're not by any means a moron."

Her tell-tale face brightened. She gave me a wan smile.

"I think I do trust *you* . . . really. You've such honest eyes. They always show what you're feeling. They can flash green fire, but mostly they're kind . . . and you look at me as you look at that dachs-hund," she admitted ingenuously. "It was horrid of Angela to try to turn me against you, wasn't it?"

"And decidedly odd. I can't imagine what's in her mind."

Uneasiness, vague but disquieting, stirred in me. I was recalling Belle's atti-tude towards Angela. Perhaps Belle had always been more clear-sighted than I had. Belle had seen Angela as fiercely jealous and possessive; a menace to any girl for whom her brothers might evince affection.

Yet, it had been Angela who had thrown Katy and Aylward together. Angela's atti-tude towards Katy appeared to be bewil-deringly ambivalent. Or . . . wasn't it? Surely Angela couldn't be hoping—or planning—that some catastrophe should overtake Katy and sweep her from Aylward's path? Leaving Aylward her heir? Oh, no! I couldn't pursue that sinister train of thought.

"Let's forget about Angela till she's here," I said impulsively. "If you're feeling up to it, we'll take Berry for a run on the sands."

The air was like wine, the sun was shimmering on the water, and the sand sparkled beneath our feet. Berry raced hither and thither, pausing every now and then to roll ecstatically on a patch of strongly smelling seaweed. I had come back to him . . . so all was well with his world. I wished that my emotions could be as direct and uncomplicated.

Did I have to be "one who remembers"? Couldn't I take things as they came, with no more backward glances? For today, at least, it was good to be alive; to feel untapped sources of energy rising in me as I ran over the sands with the dachshund.

Katy, still looking and feeling subdued, preferred to bask on a dry rock in the sunshine. She lay, stretched out, chin on her hands, gazing out to sea, while I gambolled with the dog. She had taken a beating—or was expecting to take one—I thought, with a pang. She would survive it, though. At her age, one almost always survived. I had gone on nursing my mother and caring for her solicitously, during all those dreary months after I had known that Cecil was lost to me.

I had known and loved Cecil for years and years. Katy hadn't known Aylward for more than a few months. Her feeling for him hadn't had a chance to become deep-rooted. To me, it looked like a girlish dream, a fond illusion, rather than a genuine, all-consuming passion. If it had gone deep, would she be so eager to talk about it? In my experience, it was normal to display surface scratches and bruises to one's friends—but pride bade one conceal a mortal wound; pride and the instinct for self-preservation.

To lick one's wounds in secret wasn't merely an injured animal's instinct. Just as a wild animal would plunge into a thicket, so would a sensitive girl withdraw herself from her usual circle. By that reasoning, I didn't have to worry unduly about Katy.

Her heart wasn't involved. She merely imagined that it was . . .

Was that a fair, impartial view of the situation? Or was I struggling to quiet my own conscience? Had I spared a thought for Katy when Aylward had rung me up last night? Had I been deliberately deceiving myself in all those years when I had paired off with Cecil? Had I accepted him as my portion, and not allowed myself to admit that he was a second-best? If Aylward was out of my orbit, had I reasoned that I could be happy as his friend and sister-in-law?

Probably, I could have been . . . and would have been. That was the ironical part of it. Had Cecil married me before he'd gone to Canada, I should have remained completely loyal and devoted to him. I should have kept my eyes fast closed to his flaws. It had been Miss Henrietta who had taught me to probe beneath the skin; to perceive and discriminate.

"Anyone would think you were about ten years old," Katy said, with a tinge of envy in her tone, when at last, breathless, I dropped down on the rock beside her.

"What's the idea of all that racing around?"

"Sheer joie de vivre—or a sense of escape, I suppose," I said, consideringly. "Suddenly, it's wonderful to be alive and free and independent."

"Are you? One can't really be free and independent without money," she demurred.

"An illusion, perhaps, but a pleasant illusion," I murmured, lying back with half-closed eyes and letting the sun caress me.

An illusion indeed, I realised half an hour later, when Katy murmured plaintively that she would like some tea. I sat up, reluctantly, and whistled for Berry, There was no flurry of scampering feet, wagging tail, and wet nose in response. I stared blankly around the deserted cove. Berry had vanished.

I called and whistled in a sudden panic. Katy eyed me perplexedly.

"Why worry? He knows his way home, doesn't he? Perhaps he has already gone home."

"Not without me. He wouldn't have left me . . ."

"He was heading for the cliffs, the last time I noticed him."

"Oh, heavens! He must have been chasing a rabbit. There's a rabbit warren, high up above, where there's sand and turf. That's why Miss Henrietta would never let him run loose on the cliffs . . ."

In a flash, my delicious sense of euphoria had vanished, to be replaced by fear and guilt. I had always considered that Miss Henrietta was unduly fussy over Berry. Whenever I had taken him for a walk, I had invariably allowed him to run loose, except in the road. I might have guessed that, once I had stopped playing with him and left him to amuse himself, his keen nose would scent the presence of rabbits. Dachshunds were natural, born hunters.

"Why are you so agitated? He'll come back, won't he?" Katy asked impatiently.

"If he can. Sometimes a dog wriggles down a rabbit hole and can't back out again."

I could have kicked myself. Hadn't I learnt by now that just one minute's carelessness or lack of attention could lead to hours of misery and vain regret, where

225

children or animals were concerned? How many mothers had suffered agonies of remorse when small children had gone missing? One read of such cases in the newspapers every week.

Missing pets weren't given the same publicity, but even so one read of dogs which had fallen down old shafts or wells or over cliffs, and of cats which had been shut inadvertently into deserted buildings, or frightened up trees from which they hadn't the nerve to descend. Cats might have nine lives, but I had never heard that dogs had, and Berry, though nearly two years old, was still very much of a baby in hard experience. He could so easily have got himself trapped in a burrow, wedged in and suffocated by a sudden fall of sand.

I did try to keep calm and not to panic, but, as that nightmarish evening wore on, my nerves and emotions became increasingly ragged. It was Alistair who, when darkness had fallen, put a stop to my feverish searching.

"See here, m'lass, you'll not help yon wee beastie by making yourself ill," he said firmly. "There's no more you can do before daylight. Get you to bed and be fresh for the morning."

"Miss Henrietta left him to me—and I've failed her. How can I go to bed when he may be suffocating? He must be terrified, anyway, if he's alive. He has never been out alone at night before."

Alistair checked my hoarse, barely coherent protests, by a finger laid across my lips.

"He'll not die of fright. Maybe he's frightened and exhausted, but hunger'll give him new energy by and by," he said with conviction. "Many a Jack Russell terrier has surfaced again after days underground."

"Yes, I know, but Jack Russells are tougher than pedigree dachshunds."

"Maybe. Maybe not. Pull yourself together, lassie! You're scaring the wits out of your patient here. She's afraid you've taken leave of yours."

He jerked a hand significantly at Katy, who was huddled up in an armchair, watching me apprehensively.

"Sorry!" I said perfunctorily.

In the mirror over the sitting-room mantelpiece, I caught a glimpse of my dishevelled and haggard self. I did, indeed, look quite distraught. My face was nearly as smeared and scratched as my hands. I had been crawling along paths and ledges, amidst gorse and bracken, trying to peer into that honeycomb of rabbit holes along the cliff face. To Katy, who'd never owned a dog or a cat, or known what it was to care for anyone or any living thing smaller and weaker than herself, I must have seemed half-crazy.

"Go and have a wash and cleanse those scratches thoroughly," Alistair ordered. "Then, you can at least swallow a bowl of soup and some biscuits."

I nodded dumbly. There was concern in his tone, but I fancied that his sympathy lay with Katy rather than with me. According to his standards, I was, for the second time in twenty-four hours, failing in a nurse's duty towards her patient.

He was right, I supposed wearily. Fear and remorse were selfish emotions. To let them take one over was a form of self-indulgence. I should be displaying more self-control. Yes, but I hadn't realised until this evening just how closely that small brown dog had twined himself around my heart-strings.

Obviously, there was no more I could do for Berry that night, except to leave a door open for him. To go on searching the cliffs in the darkness would be highly dangerous as well as futile. I trailed upstairs to the bathroom. I couldn't remember how I had incurred so many scratches. I might be "looking like the village blacksmith's daughter". I certainly wasn't looking or behaving like a professional nurse.

I was bone weary and heart-sick to the verge of tears. I had an absurd yearning for a broad shoulder on which to rest my throbbing head, and for strong arms to hold me comfortingly. I was, I supposed, longing nostalgically for my father. I couldn't remember that Cecil had ever offered me much in the way of physical or emotional support.

Alistair might disapprove of my obsession with Berry, but he was kind enough when I rejoined him and Katy. So, in a gauche, embarrassed fashion, was she. They made me sit beside the fire and drink a bowl of Martha's warming broth. I'd barely finished it before Martha herself appeared with cups of steaming hot chocolate and some newly baked ginger biscuits.

"Mustn't give up hope yet, m'dear love," she admonished me. "Our Abraham's been away for days and come back safe and sound, as well you know."

"Yes, but cats do wander . . . Tom-cats, that is. Dogs are different," I said unhappily.

"Aye, but he's young and agile. If so be he's down a rabbit hole, he'll wriggle out of it when he gets back his nerve," Martha said soothingly. "You're sure he didn't wander off to the village?"

I shook my head wearily. Katy and I had searched the village hours ago, and made virtually house-to-house inquiries. Most of the villagers knew Berry by sight, but not one of them had spotted him today. I didn't think he would have gone that way alone. He tended to be nervous of strangers; of anyone in fact except his immediate circle. Even as a puppy, he hadn't been indiscriminately friendly.

"Well, he's several sizes bigger than a sparrow. Put your trust in the Lord and try for a good night's rest," Martha admonished me. "And you, too, young missy. You're looking fair peaky again."

"Yes. Time you were in bed, Katy," I began.

Then, a sudden overwhelming feeling of drowsiness swept over me. I should have dropped the cup of chocolate had not Alistair moved forward swiftly to take it from me.

"*You*—" I said, blinking at him accusingly. "You've given me something . . . in that soup, I suppose . . ."

"Only a mild dose . . ."

"Mild? It feels like knock-out drops. You shouldn't . . ."

I wanted to flare at him; to tell him that, as I hardly ever took even aspirin, any kind of sleeping pill would be only too effective, and that he shouldn't have given me anything without my consent. Only . . . my tongue seemed reluctant to function and my eyelids were closing.

"Come on, now! We'll get you up to bed."

I was vaguely aware of being hauled to my feet and of stumbling to the door. Alistair must almost have carried me upstairs. My legs seemed to be encased in lead. Odd, I thought drowsily, as I sagged against him, that some physical contacts could mean so little and others so much. Alistair might have been old Martha for all the response his firm clasp aroused in me.

Perhaps I had developed an immunity. I couldn't even feel embarrassed as he and Katy helped me to undress. I couldn't feel anything beyond this overpowering, numbing drowsiness.

Before I finally sank into oblivion, I heard Alistair ask concernedly: "Will you be all right?"

I managed to mumble: "No thanks to you. Leave the side door open for Berry," but I wasn't sure if he had heard me.

With a desperate effort, I pushed my eyes half open. Alistair wasn't looking at me. He had turned away from the bed and was bending towards Katy, who was gazing up at him with a sweet, trusting smile.

It didn't have to be an oak, I thought hazily, letting my heavy eyelids close again. A sturdy Scots fir would probably suit ivy equally well.

14

"Yes, call me by my pet-name! let me hear
The name I used to run at, when a child."

ELIZABETH BARRETT BROWNING

"YOU were furious with him last night, but you look a lot better this morning, after your sleep," Katy said naïvely, over the breakfast table. "He was quite right to give you that sleeping tablet, wasn't he?"

"I suppose so," I conceded grudgingly. "It wouldn't have helped Berry if I'd lain awake. It was high-handed of Alistair, all the same. He should have asked me . . ."

"You would have refused to take it," Katy said, with one of her flashes of perception. She smiled dreamily. "He is masterful, but . . . wonderfully kind, too. He doesn't make one feel a fool, like Cecil does. Do you know what I mean?"

"Alistair is a positive, forceful character.

233

He doesn't need to blow up his own ego by deflating other people's egos," I nodded.

Cecil hadn't been as tough or as virile or as attractive physically as his elder brother and sister, I remembered. Hence his clinging to his sobriquet of "Mr. Brain". Alistair was an only son, with several adoring younger sisters, I'd gathered. Alistair had never known the urge to compete; to demonstrate his superiority. It was that urge, of course, which would impel Cecil up the ladder.

"I think he's a dear." She hesitated, then blurted out: "Would you mind if I went to Land's End with him this morning? I've never been there, and he said the drive would do me good. He has to visit an old patient who's living quite near there. He said we could have a picnic lunch afterwards, on the headland. It would be fun . . ."

"Go ahead, by all means."

"You're sure you don't mind? I'd stay if I thought I could help, but Berry hardly knows me. If he comes to anyone's call, it'll be to yours," she said earnestly. "Alistair said I would be more hindrance than help, because heights turn me dizzy, and I might slip on the cliffs. He thought you would be relieved if he took me off your hands."

"Go ahead," I repeated, "but . . . be careful. Don't begin to glamorise Alistair. He's a down-to-earth character."

"I know that." She flushed. "You think I'm an idiot child, don't you?"

"No. Merely young and romantic and lonely. I've been there before, when I was younger than you are." I sighed. "There are some girls who can cheerfully stride off on their own. The rest of us yearn for someone to walk beside us . . . and we don't always wait for the right yoke mate."

She looked at me as if she were about to repeat her observation that I didn't "talk like a nurse" or "like the village blacksmith's daughter". Instead, she sprang up, came to my side, and gave me a quick, awkward hug.

"You're a dear. You do understand," she murmured. "He—Alistair—says the vital thing is not to wallow in the dust after a fall, but to scramble up and try again. He says I haven't been giving myself a fair chance."

I smiled at her, wondering how long the "Alistair says" mood would last. It was a change, at least, from "Angela says . . ." and a change for the better. What Alistair told her would undoubtedly be sound common sense.

"So long, then. I'll be back long before Angela and Aylward can arrive," Katy added. "I do hope Berry will turn up again. I suppose he couldn't have been stolen?"

I shook my head. I had dismissed that possibility last night. Berry was far too wary of strangers to have put himself within grabbing distance of anyone he didn't know. I had rung up the nearest police station on the remote chance that he could have strayed, but I was virtually certain that he was still somewhere on or in the cliffs.

In a way, as Alistair had anticipated, it was a relief to have Katy "taken off my hands". All the same, I felt horribly alone, after she had driven away with Alistair. Martha was sympathetic enough, but she couldn't crawl about on the cliffs at her age. A missing child would have had every able-bodied person for miles around out searching, but I couldn't expect people to turn out to look for a missing dachshund. Berry was my dog, and it was up to me to rescue him.

The night's rest had helped. I could control my impulse towards blind panic now. I could even keep some hold on my over-active imagination, and try to use my intelligence. The cliffs might be honey-combed, but all the holes visible weren't accessible to a dachshund. Nor were all the ledges which led to some of them. Quite a number of them were in the possession of nesting seabirds, too. I couldn't visualise the highly-strung little dog's braving the fury of aggressive gulls. Gulls could be very fierce indeed.

I would go down to the cove again, I decided, and try to pretend I was Berry. I would work my way slowly up the path, exploring every side track which he could have negotiated, but ignoring those which would have entailed a flying leap. Dachs-hunds were less agile than terriers. They hadn't a great deal of spring in their comically short legs.

If only I could catch a glimpse of Berry's tail or hear his whimper, I could surely enlarge the hole enough for him to wriggle out of it, but the morning wore on without any sign of him. Hot and dusty, I crouched by rabbit holes, listening with strained ears, and calling "Berry!" repeatedly.

If he was alive, why didn't he make some sound? Had he barked or whimpered himself hoarse during the night, while I had lain helpless in a drugged sleep? Had he suffocated—or at least lost consciousness? He might have stunned himself in his struggles to escape. He might be too exhausted or too terrified to go on struggling. The constant mewling and whirring of the seabirds was fraying my nerves. Did they have to circle over me with their mournful cries? I had an absurd feeling that they were willing me to fall. I had no illusions about them. I had seen what they would do to a carcase, or even to a sickly new-born lamb.

I nearly did slip from a narrow ledge from sheer shock when I heard my own pet name called. I had taken it for granted that Angela and Aylward wouldn't reach Port Mathers before tea-time. I grabbed at a handful of bracken roots to steady myself, wriggled sideways, and blinked dazedly up at Aylward. He was standing at the head of the path, leaning on a stout stick. The sun was blazing down on the rich dark brown of his hair, just as in my first glimpse of him, all those years ago, and I felt the same excited quickening of my pulses.

"Conker!" he called again. "Break off for a minute or two, love! Angela wants to talk to you."

I squirmed back to the path, and scrambled to my feet, trying futilely to brush the dust and bits of dead bracken from my slacks. This wasn't how I would have chosen to meet Angela again. I felt irritated and at a disadvantage.

I said accusingly: "You didn't warn us that you would get here so early. We didn't expect you till tea-time."

He reached out his free hand to me—to haul me up to the top of the cliff. The firm grip of his fingers was poignantly familiar . . . but I had never seen those fingers so pale before. The sight gave me a painful pang.

"You have Angela to thank for that. As usual, she's in a tearing hurry. She had me up and loaded aboard by six o'clock this morning," Aylward said resignedly. "She's planning to dump me here—and take off for Plymouth."

"For Plymouth? Why?" I asked blankly.

He shrugged his shoulders. They were still pleasingly broad, but he had lost weight. His sports jacket hung loosely on him, and he'd had to belt in his terylene slacks.

"Angela's in the house, freshening up. She'll explain," he said, tucking my hand through his arm. "No sign of the dog? That's tough! The old lady told us you were out here, hunting for him. When did he vanish?"

"Yesterday afternoon. I feel so awful about it, because Miss Henrietta never let him run loose. It's as though I've failed her as well as Berry . . ."

All my pent-up misery and remorse came spilling out unashamedly. I had never had any reservations where Aylward was concerned.

"If you had asked him, he would have gladly taken the risk. It's not much of a life to be kept on the leash all the time," he said comfortingly. "Don't lacerate yourself! It's amazing how long a dog can survive in a rabbit burrow, or down a mine shaft. With any luck we'll find him. Berry? Why?"

"Brown as a berry! Miss Henrietta used to say that was a ridiculous comparison, because most berries are red or black. We came to the conclusion that it could mean coffee berries, but they're really beans. You would have liked Miss Henrietta, Aylward."

"Naturally—if you did," he said easily. "Hasn't it ever dawned on you, Conker, that we're two of a kind? Like a pair of gloves?"

"No. I hadn't thought of it," I said dazedly.

"To paraphrase Kipling, my version runs:

'You like the things I like,
And you see the things I see,
And what I think of the likes of you
You think of the likes of me,'"

he quoted. "Isn't that the way of it, Conker?"

"Is it? Perhaps," I said confusedly.

When he looked down at me with that familiar, heart-warming smile, and said "Conker" in that caressing intonation which was peculiarly his, I was as powerless to argue with him as I had been years ago. He was limping perceptibly as we moved towards the cottage, there were fresh lines around his mouth and eyes, and he had lost some of his exuberant, youthful sparkle, but he was still Aylward, my friend and hero. He hadn't changed in any of the ways that mattered.

"I just wanted to get things straight. I know you can't think of anything now except your Berry," he said apologetically. "We can talk later. Only, don't let there be any more misunderstandings . . . any more spiders' webs."

"Spiders' webs?" I echoed in bewilderment.

His lips twisted wryly.

"Angela can't help weaving webs. She has a genius for intrigue. I suppose it comes naturally to people who are born with a yen for power. They have to achieve their own ends, no matter by what means." He paused, then added: "We're not identical twins. You knew that, of course?"

"Did I? I've forgotten. To look at, you're remarkably alike."

"We used to be," he amended.

I didn't know what he meant by that. People didn't change basically in their looks. He and Angela would always be tall and dark and handsome.

As if aware of my perplexity, he said: "It's inevitable that some people should grow apart . . . grow in different directions. Ambitions take their toll and leave their mark. Didn't you notice that, when you saw Cecil again?"

"Cecil? Oh, yes!" I was oddly loth to discuss Cecil. "He already has the stamp of prosperity and success."

"Were you surprised?"

"Not really. He was a clever little boy —and greedy."

We had almost reached the side-door when it swung open and Angela came out at full speed.

"Oh, there you are, at last! Come on in now," she ejaculated imperiously. "The old girl's laying on coffee and sandwiches. I must take off again as soon as I've had

243

a snack and collected that idiot child. I gather that she's at the doctor's."

I had an absurd feeling that she was a destroyer, bearing down on me at full steam ahead, and that I was merely a small sailing boat, liable to be cut in half if I impeded her progress. Then, Aylward's fingers tightened over mine—and I jerked up my chin.

"Hello, Angela!" I said, quite calmly. "If we had known you would be here by lunch-time, I'm sure Martha would have been pleased to offer you a meal. This is her house now."

"So your last job didn't pay dividends?" she said amusedly. "Not very adept at picking them, are you, Connie? Still, if it led to a worth-while husband, it wasn't a dead loss. According to the stop press news, he's an up-and-coming young lawyer."

I met her half-scornful, half-challenging glance and realised instantly what Aylward had been trying to convey to me. This wasn't the Angela, the gay, reckless, imperious but fascinating leader, of our schooldays. This was a cut and polished stone, diamond bright and diamond hard.

Everything about her, from her carefully artless hairstyle, to her exclusive tailor-made, wild-silk shirt, and hand-made shoes, spoke of money and success. Angela was further up the ladder to fame and fortune than Cecil had yet climbed, I sensed, but she had forfeited even more than he had, during that arduous progress.

"You're way ahead of me," I told her. "Or your information service is."

"Hasn't he come to the point yet? Hang on, and I dare say he will," she said lightly —and, in a flash, at last, I understood why Belle had resented and withstood Angela.

That tone of patronage was insufferable in its casual, couldn't-care-less fashion. Even as a child, had I been her contemporary, I must have rebelled against it. As it was, I had never tried to meet her on equal terms. I had been content to trail after her, with her brothers.

Cecil had evidently escaped from her dominance, though I suspected that he was influenced by her, and her standards. Was Aylward still her loyal subject?

"Well, come on and feed! I've no time to lose," she said impatiently. "We have to be in Plymouth before four, to meet Harry's yacht when it docks."

"Harry?" I repeated.

"Harry Haylett. The idiot child's fond papa." Her carefully shaped brows drew together. "Why did she go to the doctor's? Why didn't he come here to see her? You should have had her treated as a private patient."

"You misunderstood Martha. The doctor had to visit someone near Land's End, and Katy went with him for the ride."

"How odd! And how inconvenient!" Angela's slim figure expressed disapproval in every taut line, as we followed her into the sitting-room. "Why did you let her go, when you knew we were coming? You've been hired to look after her. A pretty poor show you've put up, too—letting her attempt to kill herself!"

"That's enough," Aylward interposed quietly. "It's not for you to take Conker to task."

"Oh, let her say what she pleases! It doesn't worry me," I told him—surprised to discover that it was the truth.

The days when I had quivered beneath

Angela's wrath, flinched at the whiplash of her tongue, and sought assiduously to win favour in her eyes, were the days of long, long ago. I had been fascinated by her then, but it hadn't been a lasting enchantment. She wasn't attempting to charm me now. I doubted if she would have succeeded, anyway. She had turned and was looking at me appraisingly, as if at a potential opponent. Her gaze swept over my dusty, scratched, dishevelled self—and suddenly she smiled; a feline smile of satisfaction.

"No, I don't suppose Katy does matter to you much, if you're planning to get married soon," she said condescendingly. "It wouldn't have been exactly pleasant for you, though, if it had been published abroad that a patient of yours had committed suicide. Harry Haylett would have cut up rough—and he's a VIP, remember."

"You misunderstood me. I wasn't implying that I didn't care what happened to Katy. I do care, and I'm doing what I can for her. It wasn't I who gave her those sleeping tablets and advised her to take them," I countered.

"It appears to have worked out well enough. It'll put the breeze up Harry—and he'll have to forget his objections to Aylward as a son-in-law," Angela observed complacently. "It's ridiculous for Harry to protest that Aylward's too old for her. That idiot child needs an older man to look after her. Besides, she's crazy about Aylward, and she'll be blissfully happy, queening it at the Hall."

Aylward and I were still standing close together, my hand clasped in his. At that, in an uncontrollable impulse of recoil, I freed myself.

"Do sit down and make yourselves at home! I'll just have a wash and see if Martha needs any help with the sandwiches," I said—and fled.

By the time I had washed, run a comb through my hair, and brushed the dusty soil from my slacks, Martha had carried in the tray and was being graciously thanked by Angela. The old charm was still there —when Angela cared to exert it—I perceived. Martha retreated, looking flushed and gratified, and instantly Angela's smile faded.

"You'd better have second thoughts, my

dear brother," she said, a whipcrack in her voice. "Your TV image will scarcely be enhanced if the rumour begins to circulate that you've given that child a raw deal; that you used her to wangle a contract from her papa and then left her cold when the contract petered out on you."

"Will you please stop trying to enmesh me?" Aylward's voice sounded weary, but firm. "You wangled that contract, as you put it. You bewitched that child and tried to hurl her at me. You made her believe that I was interested in her."

"Well? You didn't contradict me. You allowed—if you didn't encourage—her to consider herself engaged to you," Angela said triumphantly. "If you try to back out of it now, your name will be mud."

"Your name, too. If you choose to blacken it, I can't prevent you. Get this straight! Never, at any time, did I ask Katy Haylett to marry me. I'm not responsible for what you've cooked up between you—and I refuse to submit to blackmail."

"How d'you know what you did or didn't do?" Angela had already started on the sandwiches. She wasn't even glancing at Aylward as she reached for the percolator. "You can't even remember her—or so you've been insisting."

"I didn't remember . . . at first. Later, it seemed the best way of letting her down lightly." The weariness in his tone was more pronounced now. He was leaning against the mantelpiece, a strained look on his face. "It's no use. I'm not playing the fly to your spider. I'm not having my future planned for me."

"You're a fool. You always were. You'll never get the Hall back under your own steam," she said contemptuously.

"Do you never listen to me? I've told you repeatedly that I don't want the Hall," he retorted. "It would be the proverbial millstone round my neck."

"What Mother and I and Cecil want doesn't count?"

"Should it? Mother wasn't born at the Hall. She didn't even marry its owner. None of us was born there. We came to it by chance. We had a pleasant interlude there, I grant you, but its attractions weren't great enough to inspire me to spend the remainder of my life struggling to retain them."

"It wouldn't be a struggle with a wealthy wife."

"Thanks for your efforts on my behalf, but a man prefers to choose his own wife."

There was still no anger in Aylward's tone, but the look of strain was becoming more pronounced.

"That red-haired witch? The village blacksmith's daughter? You must be mad! Can't you see how important backgrounds can be?" Angela snapped.

"To some people. Not to me. Nor to Conker, if I know her. Why this hankering after faded grandeur? You're doing pretty well on your own. You don't need that kind of security."

"For how long can I stay at the top? It's a real rat race . . . and I haven't any special pull. If I had my studios at the Hall—"

Aylward gave a quick, impatient sigh, and involuntarily I stepped forward. Angela had her back to me, but Aylward turned his head and smiled a welcome.

"You never give up, do you, Angela?" I said. "Can't you leave Aylward alone? Can't you realise that he hasn't the show temperament?"

"What's that?" She swung round, coffee cup half-way to her lips. "Show temperament?"

"Don't you remember our ponies? It was useless trying to school those which hadn't the right temperament for shows— or for jumping, either. 'You can force a horse to the water . . . etc . . .' That's equally true of people," I said impulsively. "Did Aylward ever go around telling everyone how wonderful he was? Showing off his paces before an admiring audience?"

"He shows up quite well in front of the cameras."

"When he's absorbed in talking about his own pet subjects. Not because he enjoys being on the screen . . ."

"Simmer down, you two! Conker love, we'd better have some sandwiches and coffee before Angela scoffs the lot. Then we'll see about finding your dog," Aylward interposed.

"*Dog*?" Angela's tone was indescribable. "That's a fine excuse! Conker has lost her dog—so you can't come to Plymouth with me to put your case to our

Harry. You have to stay here to look for a dog. Heaven grant me patience!"

"I have nothing to say to Harry Haylett," Aylward told her.

"No explanations? No apologies?" Angela arched her brows at her twin. "He's not likely to offer you another assignment in a hurry, unless you can put up some kind of defence for your behaviour to his daughter."

"*My* behaviour? I didn't push the girl over a precipice."

"Do you imagine that I did?" Angela's dark eyes were flashing.

"I have no idea. Did you?" Aylward inquired. "It was your suggestion that Katy should execute a Will in my favour."

"So that's what you've been suspecting of me?"

"Not suspecting. Wondering . . ."

Brother and sister stared at each other —and it was like the clash of steel. Angela was the first to break from that long, interlocking scrutiny.

She said with less than her usual assurance: "I wouldn't have taken such a crazy risk. Someone might have seen. As a matter of fact, I was on the path above with Cecil when that boulder became dislodged."

Aylward made no comment. He simply went on looking at her.

"All right, then! I should have yelled a warning." She tossed her head restively, just as years ago she had been wont to toss back her long, heavy dark mane. "I didn't —but nor did our dear brother. Perhaps we were too startled. It all happened very quickly. The boulder almost missed Katy. It barely grazed her as it crashed past— but that was enough to make her lose her balance."

"And you two calmly strolled away, back to camp?" Aylward said incredulously.

"We left you to play the gallant rescuer," she amended. "How could we guess that you would slip, or that the mist would come down? We didn't feel like stumbling about in the mist and risking our necks for Katy. Anyway, she was lucky."

"As lucky as when she swallowed those capsules?" I thought wryly, but I didn't speak—and neither did Aylward. He just looked at his sister as if in stunned shock.

Angela's handsome features hardened.

"Your gratitude overwhelms me," she said ironically.

"What do I owe you? A long spell in hospital and a highly embarrassing situation?" Aylward's tone was unnaturally even, as though he were exerting all his self-control. "Whatever you have or haven't done has been in your own interests, not mine. You've lied to me ever since we were kids, although I didn't realise it till recently. You shouldn't have lied to that trusting child. I find that kind of betrayal unforgivable."

"You're a fool and a prig—as you always were! Go your own way, then—and see where it lands you," Angela said scornfully. "In some draughty shack in a swamp, surrounded by screeching birds, I shouldn't wonder! Conker had better think twice before she hitches her wagon on to yours."

15

"What's the best thing in the world?
Memory, that gives no pain;
Love, when, so, you're loved
again."
ELIZABETH BARRETT BROWNING

ANGELA had usually made masterly exits. On the few occasions in our early days when someone had thwarted her, she had been an adept at "sweeping out", with her forceful chin in the air, leaving us to gaze after her in acute discomfiture.

On this fateful occasion, though, her anger had overreached itself. Aylward and I glanced involuntarily at each other—and the drawn lines on his lean face crinkled into a schoolboyish grin.

"'A draughty shack surrounded by screeching birds'," he echoed, his voice shaking with suppressed laughter. "Well, that's a variation on 'love in a rose-

256

wreathed cottage'. Does it hold any appeal, my love?"

"Why not? I don't mind draughts—and I like birds . . . except the predatory kinds . . ." A fiercely burning, rapidly soaring exhilaration was taking possession of me, licking through my veins like liquid fire and filling my whole being with a wild, incredulous joy. "Are you offering me a share in your shack, Aylward? It sounds like sheer bliss to me . . ."

"You're crazy—the pair of you!"

What else Angela hurled at us as she gathered up her driving gloves and crocodile handbag, I couldn't have said. The tension had suddenly snapped, and we were grinning delightedly at each other— Aylward and I—in the old, intimate, conspiratorial fashion.

At the door, Angela paused and swung round—as if to give her twin one last chance.

"How will you like it if I marry Harry —and he instals *me* at the Hall?" she demanded. "You couldn't stop us. There are always ways and means of having a lease transferred—when one has Harry's kind of money."

"If that's what would satisfy you, go right ahead—and the best of luck to you," Aylward answered good-humouredly. "Have I ever tried to interfere with your plans for yourself? Ever since we first met Conker, you've been driving wedges between her and me—but you were no match for Fate. Having found Conker again, I shall hold on to her while there's breath in my body. What *you* do is entirely your own concern."

I could never forget how Angela looked at that moment; the arrogant poise of her shapely dark head and elegant figure, and the unquenched fiery determination in her fine dark eyes. She was more than strikingly handsome. She was very nearly beautiful. Not quite, because the emotions she was registering were too savage and primitive not to dim that inner light which illuminates true beauty.

She might have been Boadicea, about to mount her chariot and drive into battle, I thought fancifully—and suddenly shivered. I had never believed in premonitions, but fear was clutching at me with icy fingers. Perhaps it was simply the superstitious fear that might be inspired by anyone who was sallying forth to challenge Fate, but I had a horrid feeling that Angela, like Boadicea, was about to encounter not triumph but disaster.

Not being clairvoyant, my thoughts ran prosaically to road accidents, and I said impulsively: "Do take care . . ."

She laughed at that—a hard, brittle laugh—and was gone. In silence, Aylward and I waited until we heard the slam of a car door and the fierce revving of a powerful engine. It seemed a long time before the echoes faded into the distance.

Aylward sighed briefly, and I said uneasily: "I wish she hadn't gone . . . like that. Why does she have this obsession about the Hall? Will she really marry Katy's father, do you suppose?"

"Who knows? In a way, they would make a good pair. Harry Haylett is charming and ambitious, good-looking, and as hard as hell," he said wryly. "But . . . does a man like that go for his feminine counterpart?"

"I wouldn't have thought so," I said . . . and shivered again. "Aylward, I have a feeling that she's going to get hurt."

"Cheer up, love! Nothing is likely to

happen just yet. Angela had a radio message from the yacht last night, to the effect that Harry had slipped and injured his back. There'll be an ambulance at the docks waiting to rush him to hospital for an X-ray. He more or less commanded Angela to be in attendance with his daughter."

"Oh! Then he'll hardly be in a romantic mood."

"Hardly, if he has slipped a disc, as he fears. He's the kind of man who takes illness or accident as a personal affront and humiliation. He's exceedingly vain of his excellent physique. If he's in for a spell in hospital, he'll take a dim view of it."

"I wonder which hospital he'll be taken to . . ." I wasn't clairvoyant, but somehow, intuitively, my thoughts had flown to Belle . . . and the old, bitter rivalry between her and Angela.

Did I have some vague premonition that they were about to cross swords again? That this time Belle wouldn't withdraw gracefully, but would stand and fight? At any rate when, weeks later, I heard Belle's news, heard that to Harry Haylett, in his pain and mortification, my sister's serene, classic loveliness had appeared positively angelic, and that it had been "truly love at first sight, because Harry's the most fascinating man I've ever met", I wasn't even mildly surprised.

"Does it matter?" Aylward said absently, moving to the table to lift the coffee percolator. "Let's forget them! I'm afraid this coffee's cold."

"I'll make some fresh—and you haven't had anything to eat yet," I said in compunction.

"Right! As well to fortify ourselves before we resume the search," he said practically.

The search? Remorse smote me as I hurried off to the kitchen with the tepid percolator. How could I have forgotten about poor Berry, even for a few minutes? How could I have experienced that delirious, unearthly joy while he might be slowly suffocating?

Aylward hadn't forgotten the dog— although he had never even seen Berry. How could Cecil have talked as if Aylward were eager to shed his responsibilities? His family had never been fair to Aylward. . .

"What kind of dog is Berry? By

261

temperament, I mean," Aylward asked, as we sampled the fresh brew of coffee and munched sandwiches companionably. "Bold? Venturesome?"

"Oh, no! He is highly strung and easily frightened. He's nervous of strangers and terrified of thunderstorms. That's why I'm certain he wouldn't have dashed off on his own—except after a rabbit."

"We had a Jack Russell terrier like that once, when we were kids. She was brave as a lion when she was hunting rats or foxes, but scared stiff of any loud noise," Aylward said reflectively. "Is there by any chance a gun in the house?"

"A gun? You mean a shotgun?"

"Any kind of gun."

"Only Miss Henrietta's joke pistol. It was her father's starting pistol—he was a school teacher and used it for school sports," I explained. "Miss Henrietta kept it in her bedroom. She said if any young hooligans broke in on us, the pistol looked deadly enough to scare them, but in actual fact it only fires blanks."

"Splendid, provided you have some blanks."

"I think she kept it loaded . . . but . . . what good is it?"

"Sometimes, a nervous dog in a tight corner just crouches and gives up trying to escape. A pistol shot, if he's afraid of bangs, may galvanise him into action."

"Wouldn't it drive him farther into the burrow?" I said doubtfully.

"It didn't work that way with our Jack Russell. Whenever she vanished, Father used to reach for his gun and fire a shot or two into the air. That always brought her rushing back to us for protection," Aylward told me. "Worth trying, isn't it?"

"Well, yes. If you think so . . ." I was still dubious, but I was prepared to trust Aylward's judgment.

I fetched the pistol, and he retrieved his binoculars from his luggage, dumped unceremoniously by Angela just inside the cottage gate. We set off for the cliff path side by side. We weren't touching, but I had the feeling that his arm was around me, comfortingly. In spite of my protests, Aylward insisted on descending the path to the cove until we had reached a position which gave us a clear view of the cliff face.

"You're only just out of hospital and

still limping," I had reminded him. "If you were to slip . . ."

I was torn between my anxiety about Berry and my new-born sense of responsibility for Aylward and his future. If he really meant that he wanted me to share that future with him, how could I bear to let him run the least risk on my account? "To love and to cherish . . ." I thought— and the ache of love for him was almost a physical pain. "Oh, if only it can be that way!"

"This'll do. Give me the gun," Aylward said purposefully. "After I've fired, watch the left-hand side of the cliff. I'll watch the right."

Even though I was prepared for it, the sharp crack of the blank shot made me jump. I hadn't realised that it would sound so loud. It seemed to echo and re-echo around the cliff—and a swarm of seabirds rose into the air in vociferous protest.

Aylward fired three times. Then he slid the pistol into his pocket and lifted the binoculars. I was gazing obediently at the cliff face, but, except for the seabirds, no living thing was stirring on it. My eyes travelled from one ledge to another, over clumps of gorse and dead bracken and brambles, up to the springy turf at the cliff top and down again to the rocks and sand of the cove.

Then Aylward, beside me, gave a triumphant cry of: "There he is! I can see his tail . . . and his hind legs. Yell to him to 'Stay!' If he backs right out, he may over-balance and crash down to the rocks."

He lowered the binoculars and began to scramble up the path again. I called imperatively: "Stay! Berry, *stay!*" even before I, too, had spotted the wildly agitated tail.

Berry was endeavouring to squirm out on to an exceedingly narrow ledge. He might, as Aylward had instantly foreseen, topple over backwards down the cliff. There was another, slightly wider ledge beneath, for which Aylward appeared to be heading.

"Let me! He's my dog," I panted, scurrying after him.

"I've a longer reach. Just hang on to my jacket, love."

There was a brief period of agonising suspense, as Aylward crawled sideways, and then, precariously poised, reached up to the rabbit hole on the ledge above him.

"Berry! Come out, Berry!" I called desperately.

"Just a little farther . . . Come here, Berry! Good chap," Aylward urged the dog. "Steady now! I've got you . . ."

It was a sorry object indeed that I took from Aylward. Eyes, nose, and mouth were plastered with soil. It seemed a miracle that the dog was still breathing. He whimpered and tried to burrow into my jersey, quivering all over like a jelly . . . exactly as he did during a violent thunderstorm . . .

"I should never have thought of firing that pistol," I said later, when we were back in the sitting-room.

Berry, his hunger and thirst appeased, and his coat clean and shining again, was sprawled out on my lap, peacefully sleeping. Aylward was lying back in an armchair, facing me. He didn't look any the worse for that scramble on the cliffs. In fact, he looked relaxed and at home.

"One learns from experience. I suppose, to head for home and the only known security, when one is frightened or hurt, is as natural to dogs as to children," he said thoughtfully. "Perhaps part of the price of growing up and standing on our own feet is the surrendering of that kind of security."

"Nowhere to run? It's hard to accept sometimes that one is all alone," I said feelingly. "I believe that's Katy's trouble. She can't accept it. She's like ivy, searching for a tree trunk."

"That child . . ." His dark brows drew together in a pucker of perplexity. "What am I to do about her, Conker? How can I unloose the tendrils without damaging them?"

I didn't know the answer. I wished fervently that I did.

Our attention was diverted temporarily from that knotty problem by Martha, who came in wheeling a trolley of tea, cakes and freshly baked scones.

"It's early for your tea, but you had naught but a snack lunch," she observed. "And the young gentleman looks as if he needs feeding up a bit. Will I make the bed in the attic ready for him?"

I glanced inquiringly at Aylward.

"Is Angela coming back? Did she book rooms for you both at the inn?"

"No. We didn't stop at the inn. She was planning for us to spend the night in Plymouth, Katy included," he explained. "I would be very grateful if you could put me up here, and if it isn't too much trouble for Miss Martha."

"No trouble. You're more than welcome. The bed'll be short for you, maybe, but Mr. Gillard used to manage with it," Martha assured him. "My guess is that he would have put up with a lot more inconvenience to be near Nurse—and I reckon you feel the same way about it."

"Your reckoning is right on target," Aylward responded, with his old, warming smile. "Thanks no end!"

When Martha had bustled out again, he asked whimsically: "Gillard? Is that my formidable rival? The up-and-coming young solicitor? He sounds like a good catch."

"I've no doubt that many people would think so," I assented. "Would you advise me to cast a fly for a good catch?"

"If that was what you'd had in mind,

you wouldn't have scrapped brother Cecil."

"I didn't. I felt I had to offer him his freedom. I didn't guess that he would snatch at it. I was terribly hurt when he did."

"Were you? Are you quite sure? Stung, no doubt, but was it more than a nettle sting? Weren't you secretly, deep down, just a little relieved? Did you really want to spend your life climbing endless ladders at his heels?"

"I don't know," I said confusedly. "I didn't see it that way at the time. It was agony to lose touch with you all."

"With all of us?" he said, and smiled at me. "I seem to remember that, years ago, you did me the honour of making me your first choice."

"Well, yes. Naturally. Who wouldn't?"

"Thank you, my love! But . . . that was then. Now . . . you may be forgiven if you have second thoughts. It won't be a shack in a swamp, exactly, but the post I've accepted will mean living in a bungalow near the marshes, on a somewhat wild stretch of coast," he said slowly. "There will frequently be parties of visiting bird-

269

watchers, but no immediate neighbours. The nearest village is two miles away. Good riding country, from what I've seen of it. We might run to a couple of horses."

"You—you've accepted the post? Already?"

He nodded.

"After your visit to St. Cyriac's. Before that, very little had seemed to matter. It was easier to drift along and fall in with Angela's manoeuvres. She and Mother and Cecil had all talked as though it would be abominably selfish of me to go for the kind of job which appealed to me," he confessed. "When I saw you again, I knew that I had an objective to fight for, after all."

I felt the prick of unshed tears behind my eyeballs. I bent over the tea trolley. I didn't want Aylward to know just how strongly I felt about him. At least, not yet. Not until he had disentangled himself from Katy.

"If you're concerned about Katy, so am I," he went on, as if he had read my mind. "It's a mystery to me how and why she ever got it into her head that I was eager to marry her, I remember once—after we'd signed that contract with her father—kissing her good night and telling her that she was "the sweetest thing". I never dreamed of marrying her—a mere child. I was flabbergasted when Cecil and Mother rang me up to congratulate me."

"Angela's doing, I imagine. She convinced Katy that you wouldn't kiss a girl unless you were deadly serious about her," I said wryly. "At least, that's what I gathered from Katy. She's painfully naïve for her age."

"There are kisses—and kisses." Before I could guess his intention, he was out of his armchair and perched on the arm of mine. He took the tea-cosy from me and replaced it on the pot. Then his arms went round me and his lips brushed my forehead.

"That's how I kissed Katy," he grinned. "This is how I kiss *you*."

Our lips met. How could I withdraw mine? It was as if I had been starving for this very contact . . .

"Feel the difference?" he asked, raising his head at last.

"Yes. Of course. Oh, my darling . . ."

"You wanted all of us . . . the whole

271

family. I'm afraid it won't be that way—at any rate not at first. The family won't be pleased," he said diffidently. "It'll be just the two of us, my love."

"What more do I want—or ever could want?" The words seemed to burst out, as if refusing to be suppressed. "But . . . if you would like to please your family and get the Hall back again, I could help. Dear Miss Henrietta left me the rights in her novels. Everton Gillard thinks there'll be a good, steady income from them . . ."

He shook his dark head firmly.

"No, my Conker. Let's live our own life—not my family's. Why sacrifice ourselves to a white elephant of a house? Unless you yearn after grandeur?"

His fine dark eyes were both tender and teasing. Impulsively, I put my arms round his neck and lifted my face to his again.

"Our own life. . . That's all I want," I murmured.

We were clasped together, lost to the world, when I was jerked back abruptly by Katy's clear soprano.

"Martha says she's made some tea. You've time for just a quick cup before your surgery," she was exclaiming. Even

272

as I tried to free myself, the door swung open, and she uttered a long drawn-out: "*O-oh!*"

She didn't retreat hurriedly, as I should have done had I been in her shoes. She came on in, Alistair at her heels. Flushed, dishevelled, and almost too deliriously happy to feel guilty or embarrassed, I met their concentrated stares. Katy's was startled and reproachful. Alistair's was coldly disapproving.

It was Berry who broke the sudden, ominous hush. He lifted his head and barked a greeting.

"*Oh!*" Katy ejaculated, on quite a different note. "You've found the dog again. I'm so glad. Where was he?"

"Angela and Aylward arrived unexpectedly early, before lunch. Aylward thought of the gun . . ."

As coherently as I could, I explained what had happened during her absence . . . or, at least, some of it. She took the news about her father with an impatient shrug of her shoulders.

"So like Daddy! He will keep demonstrating how young and fit he is. Then, when he strains or wrenches a muscle or something, he fusses as though he's at death's door," she said, with youthful intolerance. "Angela thinks he's the tops, but she hasn't seen that hurt 'small boy' side. Hospital's certainly the best place for him. I can't see Angela in the rôle of ministering angel."

"Neither can I. Did you have a pleasant trip?" I asked, with a desperate attempt to appear at my ease. "Grand scenery, isn't it?"

"Wonderful . . . but anywhere seems lovely, in the right company . . . don't you think?" Katy directed a glance at Alistair which, to my amusement, made his colour rise hotly. "I've learnt a lot today. I'll always be grateful to you for bringing me down here, Constant."

"Good! You're looking very well. Blooming, in fact," Aylward said appraisingly.

"You've remembered me at last?" she asked—but not as if it mattered especially.

"I've remembered how we met and a good deal else—but, frankly, I can't remember that there was ever any question of an engagement between us," he answered deprecatingly.

"It was your sister's plan, really. She sort of pushed us into it . . . and it did look like a nice idea at the time. I was terribly young and inexperienced. I expect I would have gone for any TV personality," Katy said—as if speaking of a self ten years younger. "Only, that kind of glamour doesn't last and, as Alistair says, it's much more satisfying to feel that you're pulling your weight in the world."

"Much," Aylward agreed gravely—but the corners of his lips were twitching.

"And, anyway, when we went to the hospital and you recognised Constant, I saw how things were between you. I'm not really a fool," Katy said loftily. "I saw how she reacted to you—and what happened when Cecil tried to make up to her. It looks to me as if you've been that way about each other since you were kids, without realising it."

"That's uncommonly perceptive of you," Aylward said appreciatively. "I'm extremely sorry if I unwittingly gave you any other impression, but it always has been Conker for me. You could say that I was her first conquest."

"Oh, not to worry! It's all experience,"

Katy assured him kindly. "It was fun, being squired around by a TV personality, but I don't really go for birds. They're such messy, squawking, uncuddly creatures, and I'd never have the patience to crouch in a hide and watch them for hours. That's *your* thing, but it isn't mine —and it's vital to express oneself in one's own way, as Alistair has been telling me. You know, Daddy always says that you can't beat a Scotsman for good, down-to-earth common sense."

Again she cast an admiring glance at Alistair, and again his colour mounted. It was almost the first time I had seen a doctor visibly embarrassed. I found Alistair's response to Katy quite touching.

Belatedly, I introduced the two men and roused myself from my blissful bemusement to play the hostess.

"It was a shame to break in on you like this, but the strong sea air has made us madly hungry, hasn't it, Alistair?" Katy apologised, cramming a scone into her mouth with childish gusto. "Never mind! You'll have the rest of your lives together."

Aylward's eyes met mine, and the light

in his was eloquent. It was as though he had said aloud: "And even that won't be long enough for me, my love."

THE END

ROMANCE TITLES
in the
Ulverscroft Large Print Series